a Dozen *on* Denver

Library of Congress Cataloging-in-Publication Data

A dozen on Denver : stories / [edited by] Rocky Mountain News.
   p. cm.
ISBN 978-1-55591-727-2 (hardcover)
1. American fiction--Colorado--Denver. 2. Denver (Colo.)--Fiction.
I. Rocky Mountain news (Denver, Colo. : 1937)
PS572.D4D69 2009
813.008'035878883--dc22

2009014557

Printed in China by Imago
0 9 8 7 6 5 4 3 2 1

Design and cover illustration by Margaret McCullough
Interior illustrations and architectural detail photos by
Charles Chamberlin/*Rocky Mountain News*
Robert Pogue Ziegler photo by Marie Griffin/*Rocky Mountain News*
All other author photos by Javier Manzano/*Rocky Mountain News*
Four lines used as an epigraph from "HOWL" from *Collected Poems 1947-1980* by
Allen Ginsberg. Copyright © 1955 by Allen Ginsberg. Reprinted by permission
of HarperCollins Publishers.

Fulcrum Publishing
4690 Table Mountain Drive, Suite 100
Golden, Colorado 80403
800-992-2908 • 303-277-1623
www.fulcrumbooks.com

a Dozen *on* Denver

Rocky Mountain News

Fulcrum Publishing
Golden, Colorado

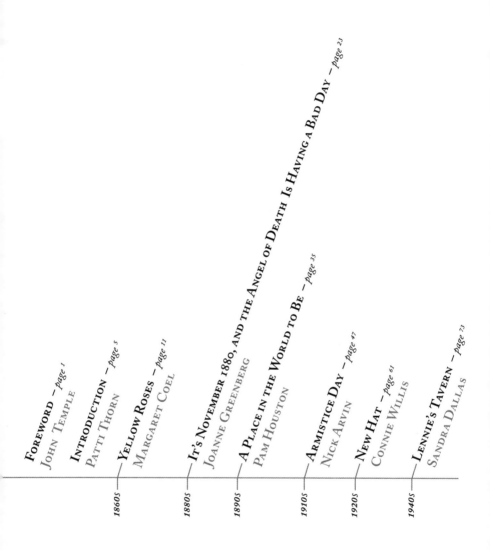

Contents

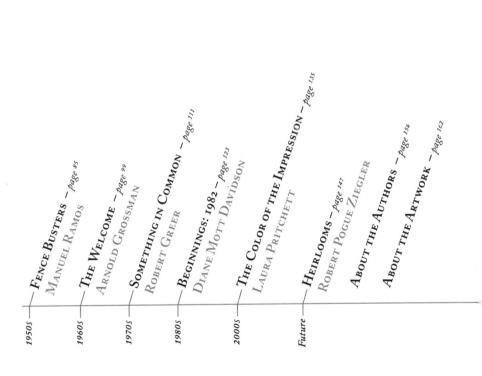

Foreword

I believe in storytelling.

While I love great journalistic storytelling, I've got to admit that fiction has a special power to tell us truths about ourselves, and our society, that are difficult for even the best journalism to touch.

That is why when I began to consider how the *Rocky Mountain News* should celebrate the 150th anniversary of the city of Denver and of the newspaper itself, I was drawn to the idea of enlisting Colorado authors to mark the two occasions. Too often when newspapers observe milestones they spend all their time looking back at their own work over the years. Readers see nothing new.

Why not, instead, celebrate the cultural richness of our community by giving some of its most creative individuals a platform to share their work with a huge audience? Why not leave behind for future generations a new set of stories casting light on how we reached this day?

The idea grew from a suggestion by Denver publishing consultant Laurie Brock, who showed me a fascinating collection of short stories commissioned by a London newspaper, *The Times*. It initially sounded relatively simple to do something similar.

Far from it, I discovered. But I'm delighted that our efforts led to a newspaper series and, ultimately, this book, including the work of eleven accomplished Colorado fiction writers and an aspiring author who won a contest to become the twelfth entry.

They are Margaret Coel, Joanne Greenberg, Pam Houston, Connie Willis, Nick Arvin, Sandra Dallas, Manuel Ramos, Robert Greer, Arnold Grossman, Diane Mott Davidson, Laura Pritchett, and contest winner Robert Pogue Ziegler. I hope you recognize some of these names. If not, you can learn more about all of them in profiles beginning on page 156.

The project wouldn't have been possible without the support of other talented contributors. I want to thank my colleagues at the *Rocky*—Patti Thorn, Charles Chamberlin, Kathy Bogan, Joe Rassenfoss, and Lesley Kennedy—as well as series managing editor Sandra Dallas, author liaison Margaret Maupin, and, of course, Laurie Brock, who guided the effort from start to finish.

I think this collection is proof that there's a place in newspapers for fiction. It's commonly said that a newspaper is fresh in the morning and fish wrap by the evening.

That's only partly true. If you visit a library and watch patrons scrolling through old newspapers on microfilm, a larger truth is revealed. Just as newspapers are a good way to find out what's going on in a city today, they also are a window to study what a community was like in years past.

The stories that make up *A Dozen on Denver* reveal something about the forces that made this the city it is today. And they are a fine way to remember the state's oldest newspaper, which sadly closed its doors less than two months before celebrating its 150th birthday. Perhaps this book will be seen as a belated present. I hope so.

—John Temple, Former Editor
Rocky Mountain News
April 2009

Introduction

PATTI THORN

DENVER HAS A LITERARY TRADITION AS BRIGHT AS ITS BRILLIANT blue skies.

It's the place where playwright Mary Chase imagined a six-foot-tall rabbit named Harvey. Where Damon Runyon honed a writing career that would eventually lead all the way to Broadway—and to the production of the perennially popular musical *Guys and Dolls*.

It's the city where Jack Kerouac and Neal Cassady forged experiences later immortalized in Kerouac's classic *On the Road*. And where William Barrett conceived his simple and poignant novel *Lilies of the Field*, a moving story that inspired the film starring Sidney Poitier.

And let's not forget Thomas Hornsby Ferril, Katherine Anne Porter, Leon Uris, Allen Ginsberg, Hunter S. Thompson, John Fante, James Michener, and John Williams—all whose lives intersected with the state, if not always the city.

No wonder when it came time to celebrate Denver's 150th birthday last year, our literary riches leapt to the forefront: what better way to honor a city than to highlight its fine storytelling tradition?

On these pages, you'll find the result of that thought: twelve stories specially commissioned by the *Rocky Mountain News* in honor of the city's birthday, as well as its own 150th anniversary (which, sadly, it never realized, falling victim to the new digital world order and closing operations just eight weeks short of its April 23rd birthday).

Inspired by a similar effort in London's *The Times*, the *Rocky* enlisted some of Colorado's most revered authors for the project, dubbed *A Dozen on Denver*. Participants included some longtime Colorado scribes as well as newer writers whose names you might not recognize, but whose work is earning increasing notice and acclaim.

Each was asked to choose a different decade of Denver's history, then craft a short story set in that era. For an added challenge, authors were also told to incorporate one of the city's most storied streets—Larimer—into their tales.

And so they did, in styles and tones recognizably their own and in stories that ran the gamut from lighthearted and amusing to those that reverberate with deeper purposes and darker tones.

The plots were as varied as their creators. The authors wrote of cowboys galloping alongside trains barreling toward Denver, and of tents pitched on the banks of Cherry Creek. They wrote of prospectors, World War I soldiers, skid row bars, pawnshops, and legendary Denver establishments such as the Oxford Hotel and Lafitte's—each story passing through, and sometimes lingering on, one key street in Denver's history.

If you read one, you can't help but dash on to the next, eager to see what other bits of history you might uncover and to revel in the burst of creativity each author brings to the task.

Interestingly, the last story, "Heirlooms," was penned not by a pro, but by the winner of a contest sponsored by the *Rocky* in which readers were asked to write a tale set in Denver's future, using the same "Larimer Street" rule. Nearly two hundred readers responded. Robert Pogue Ziegler, of Paonia, took the honors with his haunting story of a mother and daughter struggling to survive in a decimated landscape.

Like many who sent in dystopian visions of the city's future, Ziegler seemed to be subconsciously plugging in to the many economic and environmental fears besetting modern times.

I hope you'll take the time to read all twelve stories. They offer a look at Denver's history unlike any other.

And they make for a wonderful gift to the city—a new set of stories to add our shared experiences, 150 years and counting.

—Patti Thorn, Books Editor,
Rocky Mountain News
February 2009

YELLOW ROSES

MARGARET COEL

1860s

Yellow Roses

Margaret Coel

She had wondered how many days would pass before someone came to tell her what to do. It had required two weeks. Two weeks to the day that the horse-drawn wagon had carried the plank coffin out onto the brown bluffs that wrapped around Denver City. The men had dug a hole in the hard ground, lowered the coffin inside, and shoveled earth on top. She had planted a yellow rose on the mound. Then she had grasped Little Mary's hand and followed the small crowd of mourners back to the log cabin on Larimer Street that she and Jed had moved into only a month ago.

Now Tom Holt sat on the other side of the plank table that Jed had nailed and glued together. The coughing had been so bad he'd had to stop and catch his breath every few minutes. When she'd washed their clothes in the tub outside, she had found blood on the rag he used to cover his mouth.

"Have you thought on what you will do, Mrs. Salton?" Tom Holt had deep-set brown eyes and bushy eyebrows that pulled together. He set his black cap on the table alongside two porcelain cups with the other yellow rose bushes she had brought from St. Louis, sparing her own drinking water to keep them alive.

"You may call me Mary Ann," she said, trying to put him at ease. She gathered Little Mary onto her lap. *Fitting that Tom Holt was the one delegated*, she thought. She had half expected Mrs. Ericson with the stone-carved face and the gray hair tightened into a knot on top of her head. But it was Holt who had guided the wagon train safely across the plains into the gold region. Only two families in the train—the Ericsons and the Saltons—and all the rest single men bragging about how they would strike it rich, go back home, and live like kings.

At first Jed had pitched a tent for the family on the banks of Cherry Creek. But within a few days, he had given one of the go-backs eighty dollars—nearly all of their funds—for the log cabin and its contents: an iron stove in the narrow room attached to the back and an iron safe painted the dullest green that squatted in one corner of the front room. The only safe in Denver City, he'd said, as if that made the ugly thing more acceptable.

"Nothing else I've been thinking on," Mary Ann said. The door stood open, allowing the early October warmth to flow into the cabin. She was aware of the carts and wagons passing outside, the sounds of metal wheels grinding into the dirt street, and the boots pounding the plank sidewalk. "I'm afraid I don't have any plans."

"In that case, Mrs. Salton—Mary Ann..." Holt cleared his throat, making a loud, strangling noise. "I expect to organize the last train for the states before winter sets in," he continued. "Men are coming down from the mountains every day. Tired of wading in the freezing creeks trying to pan a little gold. They're wanting to go back. It'll be best for you and the child to join the train."

"I see," Mary Ann said. They had passed trains of go-backs on the crossing, shoulders hunched in discouragement, faces set in bitter lines. She had watched them pick up some of the leavings along the trail—heavy pieces of furniture that folks had pulled out of the wagons for fear the oxen would collapse before they got to Denver City. Jed had set out her mother's mahogany desk and the organ he had loved to play. She had wondered if someone would pick them up. She had never thought she would be among the go-backs.

She brushed her lips against Little Mary's silky yellow hair. Such a docile child, small fists wrapped around a cloth doll. Not yet four years old, but paying such close attention to the man across from them, as if he had parted a veil and revealed her future. Madame Sylvester's school in St. Louis would mold her into a proper young lady who spoke French and knew how to make lace. She would grow into a pinched and placid woman, like Mary Ann's own mother, who took her pleasure every afternoon at the front window watching the world pass by.

"This was our dream, Jed's and mine," Mary Ann said. They had wanted something different for the child. A new land with new

ways and possibilities. Even on the trail, the women had worked alongside the men, as if they were equals. She had loved striding beside the wagon, the swinging movement of her legs and arms, the blue sky all around, and Little Mary running ahead.

"I'm sorry for your loss." Holt was looking about the cabin, and she followed his gaze: the chinked log walls and swept dirt floor, the ugly safe claiming its space, the mattress in the opposite corner, and the barrel still packed with sacks of flour, sugar, salt and hard-tack, winter clothing, quilts and good china, the few things that had made the crossing. There had been no time to settle in when Jed was sick, and no reason afterward.

"The fact remains," Holt went on, "Denver City's a rough place, lacking in civilization. No place for a respectable woman and a little girl. Could be Indian trouble any day."

"The Indians seem friendly enough." Mary Ann had often seen Arapahos mingling with goldseekers on the streets, trading buffalo robes for tobacco, coffee, and sugar. An Arapaho village stood at the confluence of Cherry Creek and the South Platte, a short distance away. The teepees shimmered white in the sun in sharp contrast to the brown dullness of the log cabins and frame buildings going up around Denver City.

"Friendly enough so far," Holt said. "But hostile Utes killed some prospectors up in the South Park a few weeks back. Indians could go on the warpath any time. And must I mention the desperadoes arriving every day?" He tossed his head toward the opened door. "Getting drunk on Taos Lightning, shooting up the place."

That was true, she thought. Some nights gunshots had shook the log walls and frayed the muslin coverings that passed for glass in the windows. Sick as he was, Jed had pulled her and Little Mary close and shielded them with his own body. But Jed was gone now.

"Best be ready in the next few days," Holt said, getting to his feet. His fingers pleated the brim of the black cap. "Wouldn't surprise me none if the Ericson family decided to leave. Old man didn't have any luck in Clear Creek. Might be they'd have room in their wagon for you and the child."

Mary Ann dipped her head close to Little Mary's and stared at the yellow rose bushes a moment. She had brought three. One was planted on Jed's grave. She meant to plant the others in front of the cabin before she had to go back.

The child slid off her lap as Mary Ann got to her feet. She thanked Tom Holt for his trouble and showed him to the door. A warm breeze stirred up little clouds of dust along the street. The bluffs in the distance had turned golden in the afternoon sun. On the horizon, the mountain peaks, streaked with snow, floated into the blue sky. She could hear Jed's voice: *There's possibilities here like we never could've dreamed.*

She watched Tom Holt make his way down the plank sidewalk, dodging groups of men milling about, until he had disappeared past the piles of wagons and carts. Then she tied on Little Mary's bonnet and put on her own.

"Where we goin', Mama?" The child looked up at her, blue eyes and pink face filled with hope. Oh, how Madame Sylvester would change all that.

"Out for a good walk," Mary Ann said, taking the child's hand and leading her outside. Wagons clattered past, wheels kicking out sprays of dust. The air was thick with the smells of horse droppings. The sun burned through her gingham dress. They made their way through the groups of men standing about. Past two fine hotels, the Pacific House and the Broadwell House, past the drugstore and the news and periodical shop, past saloons and billiard halls and a barber shop. Some of the men tipped their slouch hats. *The widow Salton.*

Mary Ann tightened her hand around Little Mary's. What was there in such a place for a widow and a child? How could she earn their keep when all she knew was French and lace making? She might start a school, except there was only a handful of children in town and few families. She might take in laundry and sewing, she supposed, but that would bring only a small pittance. This was a place of goldseekers. How could she traipse into the mountains and pan gold with Little Mary to care for?

They turned into the confectionary shop. Mary Ann found two pennies in her skirt pocket, and Little Mary selected a peppermint stick, which she sucked loudly as they continued down Larimer, weaving through the knots of men. Wagons clanked past, and sounds of laughter erupted from the saloon in Apollo Hall. Several men were lined up in front of the Eldorado eating house on the corner. Rough and uncivilized, Tom Holt had said, and yet Denver City seemed a place of energy and possibility. They would walk every day, Mary Ann decided, until they had to leave. She would memorize every detail of Larimer Street. She never wanted to forget.

They reached the dry bed of Cherry Creek and were about to start back when Mary Ann saw what looked like a crowd of prospectors bunched in front of the two-story plank building that stood in the middle of the creek bed. A sign that said ROCKY MOUNTAIN NEWS stretched across the top of the peaked roof. Wagons were rolling in, prospectors jumping out and joining the crowd. Each man gripped a drawstring canvas bag.

She walked the child a little way down E Street until she was close enough to make out the sign on the side of the building: ASSAY OFFICE, Byers & Shermer. In an instant she understood why Jed had paid out so much of their funds for the cabin. Too ill to follow the creeks into the mountains panning for gold, he had searched for another way to earn their living. Then he'd met the go-back looking for somebody to take the cabin and its contents off his hands, and in the cabin was a safe.

She started back, pulling Little Mary along, something opening up inside her, like a rose turning to the sun. "We must hurry," she told the child. Little Mary started skipping ahead, as if she, too, sensed a new possibility.

Inside the cabin, she dropped to her knees in front of the dull green safe. The door held fast. Somehow she would have to work out the combination. She leaned in close, the way she'd watched Papa open the safe in the back room of his store countless times. She turned the knob slowly, listening for the tiny clicking sound. Ah, there it was.

She kept turning the knob. Another sound, then another. Still the door remained locked. She sat back on her heels, stung by the sharp sense of defeat, and closed her eyes a moment. She could almost feel the bounce of the wagon and smell the perspiration pouring off the oxen. They would be going back to the past, when the future was here. She glanced around at Little Mary, dancing the doll across the tabletop, her yellow hair flowing freely over her shoulders.

She got to her feet and stepped over to the small chest of Jed's things that she kept beside the mattress. Folded inside was Jed's second best shirt, the one he wore every day. She had seen that he wore his best shirt for burial. She set the shirt and a few other clothing items on the mattress and lifted out a mahogany box. She opened the lid and stared at Jed's revolver, memories tumbling through her head. They had walked along the bed of Cherry Creek a half mile or so from town, she and Jed and Little Mary, and Jed coughing so bad. He had placed the revolver in her hand. "You must learn to shoot," he'd said. "Ladies here must know such things."

She set the mahogany box to one side and drew out the canvas-backed ledgerbook. The lined pages contained the accounts of their life together, recorded in Jed's precise handwriting. The pay he had earned in Papa's store, the costs of household items and food. The last entry was September 16, 1860. $80. Log cabin and contents.

Beneath the entry was a series of numbers separated by dashes. She went back to the safe and turned the knob according to the numbers. The door sprung open. She clasped the ledgerbook to her chest, conscious of the salty tears stinging her eyes. "Thank you, Jed," she whispered.

It didn't take long—not more than twenty minutes, she reckoned—to tear four empty pages from the ledgerbook into narrow strips the size of calling cards back in St. Louis. On each strip she copied the same words with a black pencil:

KEEP YOUR GOLD SAFE!

THE ONLY SAFE IN DENVER CITY

Located on Larimer Street

Proprietor: Mary Ann Salton

She put the strips of paper in her pocket and tied Little Mary's bonnet under her chin again. "We're going for another walk," she said, guiding the child into the street. Little Mary skipped ahead, trailing her doll along the sidewalk, giggling in the afternoon sun.

Mary Ann recognized Tom Holt's footsteps on the sidewalk before she opened the door. Outside the yellow rose bushes were beginning to stand tall. Holt studied them a moment before he removed his cap and stepped inside.

"What's all this?" he said, looking about the cabin. She had hammered pegs into the log walls and hung the clothing that had been in the bottom of the barrel. A good linen cloth covered the table, and another linen cloth draped the barrel. The wood carton she'd found on the street made a satisfactory cabinet for the good china. She had made another doll from scraps of fabric in the barrel, but Little Mary seemed happier running and playing on the sidewalk. The child had insisted upon helping her plant the roses.

"We've been settling in," she said.

"Settling in? The wagon train leaves day after tomorrow. I must warn you, there's snow in the mountains. Winter is coming soon. Won't be any other trains going back. Mrs. Ericson has been kind enough to make room for you and the child, but you must leave your belongings behind."

"I thank you for your trouble," Mary Ann said, "but we won't be going back. This is our home now."

"Heard about your scheme, renting space in that safe of yours." Holt nodded toward the corner of the room occupied by the iron safe. The bushy eyebrows pulled together. "Don't see how that's gonna bring in enough to keep you alive."

"I'll be using some of my earnings to grubstake the most reputable clients," she said. "I will have a share in whatever gold they find. Other clients are wanting to join me in the investments, and I will see even larger profits for putting the ventures together. There are great possibilities in this place, Mr. Holt. Little Mary and I would be sorry to leave them behind."

Holt let out a loud guffaw. "At the mercy of the flotsam and jetsam out there?" He stepped sideways and waved through the opened door at the passing wagons, the knots of men sauntering along the sidewalk. "They'll burst in here and rob you blind."

Mary Ann moved toward the barrel, lifted the linen cloth, and brought out Jed's revolver. The metal felt cold in her hand, but not uncomfortable. "I hardly think that will be a matter of concern," she said.

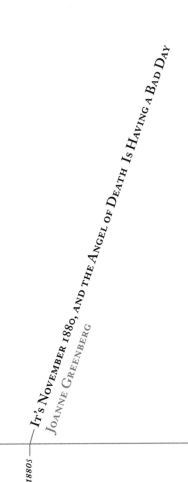

1880s

It's November 1880, and the Angel of Death Is Having a Bad Day

Joanne Greenberg

*It's November
1880, and the
Angel of Death
Is Having
a Bad Day*

JOANNE GREENBERG

THE ANGEL OF DEATH FOR THE FOUR-YEAR-OLD STATE OF Colorado has overslept. An hour after his normal waking, he heaves himself from his lumpy mattress. In the old country, he remembers with a pang, they had feather beds, deep, warm, and soft. You could lie by the chimney and...He sighs. He is in his frailer years and had dreamt yet another dream of happier times.

On the whole, here, human mortality has gone its regular, steady course. Wars, which demand the calling up of hundreds of assistants from miles away with all those logistical and personality problems, hadn't been a worry in this country since Appomattox. This year is a phenomenal year, even though its calls are nothing like those of the plague years of Europe or those that had brought him to these shores, the smallpox and diphtheria that had ravaged the continental tribes.

He is presently unmarried. His last wife had left him over the mess of Sand Creek. She had been A Curse Wife. People don't make those old Yiddish curses anymore: "May your daughter marry the Angel of Death." The Middle Ages had given him the choice of thousands of those daughters, some as crisp as autumn apples, wished on him in the airy innocence of curse-makers.

Scratching his unshaven face, he goes downstairs to check the weather and the day's assignments. These usually appear on a blank, whitewashed wall of his kitchen, the delicate fingers of a man's hand inscribing the details.

The year has been hard. The children have begun their deaths in the drafty houses of Cripple Creek and Merino, in Guffey and Fairplay, in Georgetown and Creede. The Angel likes kids. They are direct, no fuss and none of the bargaining and conditions-altering the old folks hand out. The Chinese are a problem, worse than the Italians and Irish. They all want passage home, impossible distances. There are tears and rages and undignified bargainings in difficult languages.

When he was young, the Angel struggled to know the future weeks in advance. He was serving the Russo-Polish sector then, very junior, and, as he looked back on it, annoyingly eager. Since his reassignment to America and to this very plum placement in what was just now Colorado, he had never failed to say a prayer of thanks for his good luck. The population here was small, the spaces wide, the scenery beautiful, the climate ideal. Even the native populations had never made permanent settlements here, so long-laid intergenerational squabbles were few, as were the tiresome demands for precedence and pretentious display. There were no untruthfully remembered glories. The people here were as sharp as the air.

There had been an uprising against the Chinese, with deaths, this year in Denver. Men were hanging from lampposts, reminding the Angel of past times and distant cities. The deaths in no way equaled those in the mines from bad air and no safety precautions, but they were more terrifying with the sudden, acute knowledge of the capacity of the animal in mankind to run mad.

He had a collection of outfits with which to comfort the dying. He had procured the Chinese round hat and long gown on Wazee Street. The newspapers reported that the Jews out here were building a hospital. It would be a blessing. Of course, his interest was not centered in how many people would be saved by such an institution, but he wasn't getting any younger, and with the Encounters taking time and all the indignation and bargaining so many of them went through, it would be a far more comfortable location to work from than the streets and the doorways in the din of horse and cart traffic and the footfalls of this restless, aggressive people.

Twenty-five today: two Chinese, placer miners in Fairplay, from a fight over a gambling game, one in an hour; fifteen kids here and in Central City and Georgetown of illness; six accidents; one hemorrhage; one female, age fifty-six, on Larimer Street.

He breakfasts on cold biscuits left over from a weekly baking. His meal is, as usual, disturbed by the falling of insects and tiny spiders that have caught his breath. At his feet a mouse lies dying from the touch of his slipper in the closet the previous night. The situation is worse in summer, but it pays him to concentrate on the contents of his plate.

He eats, then goes back upstairs, chanting quietly, showers, shaves, dresses, then comes down again ready to begin his work. In his suitcase are the garbs and appearances that bring comfort, or at least familiarity, to the Encountered—there's the gray cloak, the fold-up scythe, the Chinese things, the eagle feather outfit. With another sigh he opens the door and steps out into the street.

It's bone cold. People huddle in coats and shawls, mufflers and muffs. The breath pours from their mouths in vapors, although, no one notices, not from his. He twists himself into a slit in the air and is away to his first Encounter.

He follows the route of the old Spanish trail up Mount Vernon Canyon past the place where the five Utes, lost in the storm, had built a snow cave back in 1804. He had taught all of them pinochle and they had died, one by one, playing happily with him until their moments came.

Fairplay and the Encountered: one does the usual carrying on about being delivered home to Canton. This costume—the long white beard, the long scholar's gown, and a white braid, hip length—saves the day. He speaks Cantonese well, but these miners have developed some new expressions and he takes the time to learn them.

Granby is next: a little girl. "It's all my fault..." She's not crying now, but she has been. "Mama told me not to play in the snow." Costume change: none. She seems to like the old Chinese man very much. He likes it when they take his hand. Now come Gothic and two kids. He takes them on a sled down a hill always forbidden to them because of the rocks and fall-off places. They thank him as he sends them on.

The woman in childbirth pleads, begs, bargains, and then gets angry. There's a husband and children. "You promised me last time I would live. Why destroy us now?"

"I'll do this for you: I won't take the baby. That way, your husband and the others will have something to work on, to save."

"But he has trouble with liquor—he'll use it for his pain and later for his excuse. I was holding the world together; didn't you know that? I'm needed here."

"I don't make the list."

It's late afternoon when he returns from the accident in Creede, and he's feeling distinctly out of sorts. Breakfast had been insufficient, and there was no place to pick up a snack between any of his far-flung meetings. His position as Angel of Death has its share of liabilities, too. More than insects die without plan. Yesterday he had stroked a cat absentmindedly and ended its life on the spot. Calling at a ranch one day for a meal, the rancher's wife had brushed his shoulder as she served him. What a bureaucratic mess that had been, not to mention his genuine sorrow at a moment that had made a family's generosity turn tragic.

Who this Larimer Street person is and what the Encounter is like will determine his evening. Sometimes there are notes on the wall about long-term illnesses, exceptional circumstances, last-minute corrections, but there had been nothing this morning but name, age, time, and place.

He has an hour to wait before the Encounter, which has been set for the almost-twilight of this icy and miserable day. He has appeared all over the state: sunny Granby; Creede, with the blue-purple snow reflecting back into the deep bowl of a liquid blue sky; Georgetown, where it had been snowing; Merino, where it had not yet begun to snow.

Here, an acid fog is lowering. The coal this city burns isn't the hard, clean anthracite of eastern cities, but a local coke, a greasy, gritty product that people hawk up mornings or as they stand on corners, in the cone made by street lamps fighting the fog.

Against this expectoration of cigar juices, coal dust, and cheek-wad, women baste long strips of cloth around the bottoms of their skirts and, on the warmer days, stay off the mud-melting roads entirely, if they can. Here and there, even on a large, populous street such as Larimer, the smell of the rotting corpses of small stray animals and the effluvium of the seldom-collected garbage hang in the air.

There is less of that penetrating odor now that most of the detritus is frozen, but people hurry along because the cold is so penetrating. The Angel stands looking down the length of Larimer Street, from which even the shining ramparts of the mountains to the west have been blotted out by the fog.

Larimer Street is wide, sided with substantial brick buildings, and, during the day, rattling with the business of the city. Now, weather and the oncoming twilight have modified the uproar, although drays, carts, carriages, and foot traffic still move on it. The Angel chooses a line of travel close to the edge of the wooden walkway, where he is unlikely to touch or be touched by anyone. At Fifteenth Street, he pauses in front of Monk and Strapper's jewelry store. What kind of adornment is fashionable now? He, himself, has sported many jewels, rings, stickpins, belts, even a baldric now and then. When necessary, in dealing with royalty, for example, he wears a crown. The children like to see him in a crown. He doubts that Monk and Strapper's will have them for sale.

Ah, wait—here she comes. He sees her from a block away, with that preternatural knowledge he sometimes has so that even in the rain, fog, or oncoming darkness he is able to pick out the anticipated one.

She's a small, tight woman, determinedly breasting a flow that is mostly moving the other way. She's in black, standard outerwear here for winter clothing, but this looks thin, and as he sees her more clearly, he's aware that much of the coat is worn and threadbare and has the grayish look of its contact with a charcoal burner and brushes against rough inner walls' lath and plaster. In the old country, even its poorest tried for a distinguishing scarf, a ribbon, some cheap adornment to set them aside from the utterly destitute. Here, too, among the tribes, there would be wrist feathers, a quill chest piece, fringes on a woman's garment. She is like a black bat, pulling darkness to it. He stands, waiting, and she approaches, but he sees with surprise that she's not walking to pass him. "Beth..." he says, putting out a hand in greeting, at least to identify himself. She's stopped before him, bristling.

"Where the hell have you been? I've been stood up for a year, a whole year, while you were plucking the low branches, collecting children!"

"Beth..."

"Beth nothing. Do you know what your incompetence has cost me? My relatives got wise. I had had them all lined up to get me through this last year in style. Will I be dying in a good, warm place, dry, clean? I live in a shanty by the river. There are rats there, and garbage, and it's all because of your blundering. You know I have consumption. You know I have a rheumatic heart. What were you waiting for, cancer?"

"I can take you now," the Angel says, wondering how he has been put on the defensive.

"Here? On the street? Are you insane? It's freezing here!"

"We might go to your cousin's place; it's only a few blocks away."

"You don't think I've tried that? They shut the door in my face. I heard the lock snap."

"Isn't there some group—what about a church?"

She cuts him off with a "prrt" of contempt. "Well?" she says, tapping her foot.

Things are tightening up. He has one other Encounter today, and time is passing. It's considered bad form not to be on time.

"Take me with you," she says.

"Impossible."

"This is America. Nothing is impossible. Take me where it's warm—what about that Chinese laundry on Wazee?"

"They'll get the blame for your body. Things have been difficult enough. Wait—I have an idea. Stay where you are; I won't be more than a few moments."

The Angel turns and glides swiftly the two blocks back to the large clothing store he noticed on his way. It is almost closing time. He turns himself around the door, carefully eluding a woman who is leaving, and who would live. The store is warm, the wood floors magnifying the sound of movement. "No Spitting" signs and the prominent placement of cuspidors keep them from becoming slippery.

The Angel lies down in the air, supine, and flows up the staircase one flight, two. The first floor had been humming with activity, but here it is all but silent. A clerk is beginning to pull dust sheets over the dresses and suits hanging on the racks. The Angel passes millinery, shoes, and there—ah—outerwear.

No one sees him glide over to the racks where the fur cloaks are hanging. He takes the heaviest one, mink, probably from skins trapped up Mount Vernon Canyon, sent to Chicago to be made up, then returned. This one is sumptuous, satin lined. He looks at the price tag: $15.95. The cost is no problem. People often press money on him. The problem now is that he is out of time.

The Angel slips the cloak on, which renders it invisible, and rides the banisters down to street level. The whole action has taken two minutes, one later than the expected Encounter. There will be repercussions from this. Before Beth Amy Miller can reopen the conflict, he whisks off the cloak and wraps it around her. She is dying, warm and dry, at the side of the store.

He stands, exhausted and disheveled, already more than brushed with the chill on the street, sorting among his marks, drachmas, lire, pesos, and rials for the price of her acceptance.

A Place in the World to Be

Pam Houston

1890s

A Place in the World to Be

PAM HOUSTON

IT WASN'T MONEY THAT HARNER WAS AFTER, AS MUCH AS A PLACE in the world to be. He'd been kicked out of several places in his short life, the first one being his father's gentleman farm just outside Scottsbluff, Neb., which, he would be the first to admit, had never been a comfortable fit, not even when he was a baby. After his mother died of influenza the winter Harner turned eleven, no amount of try on his part could earn him a place there. He got a job as a hand on a huge wheat and cattle operation just over the Colorado border but got kicked out of the bunkhouse for snoring and eating more than his share of the food. Then he drifted west and took up with a lonely widow in Cheyenne, but she kicked him out when, despite the fact that at seventeen he was twenty years her junior, he could not be aroused enough times a day to satisfy her sexual appetite. His love for Katherine was never in doubt, but the truth was, she scared the scrap out of him, and when you added it all together, his father's fists and Cookie's threats and Katherine's eager, insatiable organs, he decided to head for Denver, the biggest city to which he could afford the fare, a city so big he might get lost inside it, so lost that nobody who wanted anything from him would ever find him again.

Harner's talents were few but reliable. He was a gifted horseman and had a gentle way about him that made him innocent until proven guilty in the eyes of the animals. He was a big man and could lift heavy things, and most kinds of machinery did not intimidate him. His father was a bookish and lonely man, a retired psychologist who read the works of young Sigmund Freud in the original German and had committed long passages of Emerson and Thoreau to memory. Harner had picked up a way with words without really meaning to. He could pick out a tune on the guitar and make up lyrics that seemed—to his great surprise—to delight listeners, especially women. He would have never described himself as good-looking, but he might admit to being one of those men whose ugliness was regularly found appealing.

He didn't know what kind of work he might find in Denver, but Katherine had said that the combination of his country-boy politeness, his surprisingly broad vocabulary, and his unconventional good looks made him ripe for the picking in a city on the rise. As she carefully packed his bedroll for him, adding at the last minute the heel of the roast they had eaten the night before and a swatch of cloth from one of her slips sprayed generously with her perfume, she spoke reassuringly.

"Apply for a job as a waiter at the Denver Club for starters. You'll make good tips and meet all the right people. Sing your songs on Larimer Street on Sunday morning, and when folks try to tip you, smile and say no thank you. You'll charm the pants off of somebody—or maybe the petticoats—and if you are lucky they will have enough money to make you a star."

When Harner got off the train in Union Station, it was not lost on him that he was stepping into the grandest building he had ever seen in his life. He had a hundred dollars in his pocket—Katherine's final parting gift at the Cheyenne station. He missed her, but not acutely, much in the way—he tried not to wince as the thought came to him—a boy might miss his mother. (He could almost see his father shaking his head and pronouncing Harner doomed with a couple of phrases of guttural German from his favorite psychotherapist.)

He stepped out of the train station and onto Seventeenth Street, where vendors, businessmen, families, tourists, bums, prostitutes, and con men dodged street cars and delivery wagons, horses and hacks. He wasn't half a block outside the train station when a great ruckus on the sidewalk took his attention, a gold banner stretched all the way across the street announcing the grand opening of a grand hotel called the Oxford. There were flags of all colors and carriages with fine horses parked out front and the fanciest people

Harner had ever seen outside of photographs, pouring through the hotel doors.

Harner stashed his bedroll in a storefront and slipped inside the lobby, which had marble floors, frescoed walls, silver chandeliers and stained glass, all combining to fill the room with something that resembled pure light. In the dining room, tables glistened with cut, engraved glassware and Haviland china. Down the hall was a barbershop, a library, a Western Union office, a saloon, and, finally, a door bearing the sign, "Employment Opportunties: All Levels of Experience Welcome to Apply."

Katherine had said the Denver Club, but she might not have known about the Oxford. She had also on many occasions told him to keep his eyes open, that opportunities presented themselves all the time to boys who kept their eyes open, that the secret in life was to seize upon them quickly, the way she had seized upon him his very first night in Cheyenne.

He ran his fingers through his hair, straightened his vest, composed his face into one of the versions of himself that Katherine found the most irresistible, and strode through the employment office door.

He got a job in the gentleman's-only dining room, and within two weeks he had served lunch to every banker, merchant, politico, and attorney in the city, along with Soapy Smith, Bat Masterson, and Doc Baggs, down from the mines in Leadville, fresh off the mountain and ready to make another deal.

Harner befriended Judy, the pastry chef, who made a study of the major players in town and could identify them immediately—especially the mine owners and the con men—by the cant of their strides or the bands of their hats. She knew who was trying to rip off whom and for how much, and who might get killed over it in the aftermath.

At the moment, she said, all of the talk was of Creede, where silver had been found only a year before, but in such great quantities it had made even the most seasoned gold men like Smith and Masterson sit up and pay attention.

The town was named for Nicholas C. Creede, who had prospected his way down to the southwestern part of the state to a place known then only as Willow Gap. Just arrived, he picked up a rock so full of quartz that he sunk a shaft immediately below the spot where he had found it. According to Judy, it was as absurd to dig for silver where he dug as it would be to sink a shaft in Larimer Street because you had found a silver quarter lying in the roadway. But Creede dug the shaft, and when he sized up the result of his first day's work, he cried, Great God! and Holy Moses! and the Holy Moses Mine was born.

Where Katherine had been willowy, elegant, and mysterious, Judy was quick-witted and sturdy, kind and helpful, straightforward as a calf. She had a group she ran with on her days off—"her girls," she called them—and they all took a liking to Harner, adopting him the way one might a pet. Patty, Bea, Janice, Martha, Mildred, Jolene, and Louise—they were single girls from good homes, with jobs and a little money, and they had connections to every hotel, restaurant, and saloon in Denver. It wasn't long before Harner was playing his songs to small but appreciative audiences five nights a week all over town.

For a little while it seemed to Harner that he might have found in Denver what other people meant when they talked about belonging. He was universally liked at the Oxford, he made friends with his music, and he knew without ever having to ask that if Judy tired of him and kicked him out of her small but stylish apartment, one of the other girls, boisterous Mildred or soulful Jolene, would take him in in the blink of an eye.

Sometimes, on his coffee break, he went up to the roof of the Oxford and watched the construction crews on all sides of him pounding the nails and laying the bricks that were increasing the size of the city—it seemed almost daily. The newspaper said Denver was now the third-largest city in the West, after Omaha and San Francisco, and it wasn't all that long ago that it had been a modest cow town at the foot of the Rockies. *That's what change was*, Harner thought, *an idea.*

From his rooftop perch he could watch the winter storms come roaring down over the Front Range, from Mount Evans all the way to Long's Peak, and see the fresh coat of white glistening up there when they blew on through to Nebraska.

He felt the mountains calling to him in much the same way the city had a few months earlier, and it occurred to him that maybe a big city was more like the mountains than small, sensible plains towns like Scottsbluff and Cheyenne were like either one. Both the city and the wilderness were unpredictable...they asked everything of a person and the nature of the request was always changing; they would heap you with good fortune and turn on you just as quickly. Denver had been almost absurdly good to Harner so far, but he was afraid his luck couldn't hold. Maybe he longed for a place that would test his mettle, that would ask more of him than a song, a shrug, and a smile.

By the time the short days of December gave way to the warm winds of March, the name *Creede* seemed to face him everywhere. From billboards, from canvas awnings stretched across the streets, from daily papers in type an inch high. Shop windows advertised "Photographs of Creede," "The only correct map of Creede," "Specimen Ore from the Holy Moses Mine, Creede," "Only direct route to Creede." "Wanted: $500 to start drugstore in Creede," "You will need boots in Creede, and you can get them here!" The gentlemen whose lunch he served at the Oxford Hotel dropped the word so frequently it was like an incantation.

"Pay attention to the signs," Katherine had told him. She had been right about Denver and right about the women. He didn't know if he had the gumption to make it as a prospector, but who knew what else a town of ten thousand that was growing by three hundred souls a day might have in store for him?

Judy shed one tear the morning Harner boarded the train. "You come back down here when your feet get frostbit and I'll warm them up for you," she said, good-naturedly. She did not put a hundred dollars in his pocket, nor a swatch of her underclothing, and for that Harner was grateful. At Union Station she had identified a stern-looking older man as "one-third owner of the Last Chance Mine," and Harner chose a seat in his car more for luck than for any practical purpose. The car filled up with grubstake prospectors with their picks propped on the seats beside them, men in flannel shirts and Astrakhan fur coats and top boots laced at the ankles, and one woman in a bright-colored dress who smoked with the men and passed her flask down the length of the car and winked at Harner when it reached him.

She caught a glimpse of Harner's guitar and sat on his lap and begged for a song, and before long she had the whole car singing along to *Ta Ra Ra Boom Di Ay* and *Throw Him Down, McCloskey.*

Her name was Bess and she was from Trenton, New Jersey, and she had that take-no-prisoners quality that he admired in girls who were raised back East. She had brown eyes and auburn hair that she tossed every time she hit the high notes. She was older than he was, to be sure, but less older than either Katherine or Judy.

"What's your plan when you get to Creede, stranger?" Bess asked him, and for the first time in his life he knew better than to admit he didn't have one.

He was saved by the slowing of the train, which stopped at the mouth of a canyon cutting through two slabs of brown rock more than a thousand feet high. He jumped out into two feet of mud and snow and took account of things. There was not a brick or awning or painted front in the whole town. Kegs of beer, bedding and canned provisions, furniture and raw lumber were heaped up in front of buildings that were cut from fresh pine and looked no more than several hours old. The street was full of men leading ox teams, mules, and donkeys, loaded with ore and sinking deep into the mud. Harner smiled to see the familiar blue and white of the Western Union sign—the same one in the lobby of the Oxford—in front of a building that leaned so precariously into the building beside it that they both seemed to be made out of cardboard.

He looked back down the way the train had come to see a half-circle of magnificent peaks, still deep in snow, and the mountainsides covered in pine and aspen, and behind those peaks another snowcapped range, mountains in every direction, for fifty miles and beyond. He paused at a bulletin board covered with handwritten notices: "Prize Fight at Billy Wood's on Saturday," "Pie Eating Contest: sign up at Kernan's," "Mexican Circus, April the First at Wagon Wheel Gap," and, most interestingly, "Church Service at Watrous and Bannigan's Gambling House—Sunday—all denominations welcome!"

Harner saw Bess mincing through the mud on the arm of an older man who she had said was one-fifteenth owner of the Amethyst Mine and was surprised when the words that formed in his head were "Good riddance."

If Judy had been born a man, she'd sure enough be up here, knee deep in mud with a pickax over her shoulder. Who knew where Katherine would be if she'd had a man's prerogative to "follow the signs"? What if Harner's father had ever taken his head out of his books long enough to smell the clean scent of ponderosa and sage that was just that minute whistling down the mountain?

The train sounded its whistle and began to chug back down the valley toward Wagon Wheel Gap, and Harner closed the collar of his jacket against the dropping temperature. He thought about all the people who had taken him in out of kindness, sent him on his way out of frustration. It was true that each one had taught him something. It was also true that they had set him free.

Dusk was falling and red and blue electric lights were shining in globes outside the buildings, mixing with the hot, smoky glare rising from the gambling houses, making the canyon floor look like something out of a gypsy's dream. Harner had wanted to lose himself in the hustle and surge of Denver, but this town felt more like a place for *finding*. Above the din and shuffle of town the two slabs of granite stood, impassive, unyielding in the twilight. *They* had something to teach Harner, too, and he was smart enough now to know it. He shouldered his bedroll and headed deeper into town.

ARMISTICE DAY
NICK ARVIN

1910s

Armistice Day

NICK ARVIN

Peace has come, and in the Manhattan on Larimer Street, where the menu offers steak for thirty-five cents, a chaotic, exuberant noise rises from the tables. Over the last week the Spanish flu epidemic has ebbed, and today came word of a signed armistice—soon the boys in France will be coming home! Few still bother to wear the gauze masks that the city mandated to combat the influenza, but a pair seated at a table near the front door wear theirs—white cloths tied back over the ears, covering nose and mouth.

"Someday you'll kill me," the big one says to the little one.

"Sure I will."

"That's what sons do to their fathers."

The boy looks about ten years old. His father has a deep crease fixed into his forehead, as if his mouth, frustrated by the mask, migrated upward. The boy has small, dark eyes, and he is unlikable. His father is also unlikable, however, which works out, in a sense. If only one or the other had been unlikable, they would work at cross-purposes, but as it is they project a peculiar energy together and seem, if unlikable, also singular.

They cut pieces of steak, lift their masks to put the food into their mouths, let the masks down again to chew.

Their unlikability has already impressed those at the tables around them. The two talk loudly while watching the door and the celebrating crowds that wander outside. They have a small, round table but sit nearly side by side. The father, eating left-handed, jostles his son, right-handed.

"What're you going to kill me for?"

"For picking your nose and a funny look," the boy says. He lifts his chin to speak in a curious, mock-theatrical style.

"You have a very disrespectful manner."

"If there's an apple on the ground, chances are the tree's nearby."

Men, arm in arm, pass the door singing. A paperboy casts his voice into an unnerving register, calling the headline, "THE WAR IS OVER!"

"You are assuming that you are, in fact, my son."

"I'm hoping I ain't."

"I indulge, but you may provoke me only so far."

"Your patience is legendary."

"You are a little cur."

At the nearest table sit two ladies and two men, all well dressed. One of the men, particularly wide in shoulders and chest, with a scar across his nose, glances over repeatedly.

"A son of a bitch, then," the boy says.

"I'll put you over my knee right here," the father says.

The boy lifts his mask and places a piece of steak in his mouth.

The waitress comes and looks at them and goes away.

"You should tell her that we can't pay," the boy says.

"I can pay."

The father and son look at each other. The father reaches into his jacket, draws out a wallet, opens it, peers inside.

He curses; the table goes over and crashes as he falls on the boy, knocking over both their chairs; the boy screams. All around the restaurant people stand to look. The father punches his son in the chest.

The man with the scarred nose gets there first and lifts away the father; the boy, still screaming inarticulately, slips out; the father scrambles and writhes, bellowing guttural syllables, while the man with the scar tries to pin him. The boy presses close, livid, and shouts insults.

Suddenly the boy backs away. A half second later the man with the scar stands straight up to feel the pocket of his pants. "You!" He turns to follow the boy, but the boy is gone. The man peers out the door. His wallet has been taken, and when he turns back, the father—the accomplice—has also vanished. The diners begin to

chatter again among themselves. The man looks out once more at the passing happy crowds.

2. The Phonograph

In a one-room apartment a floor above the celebration and noise, a woman sings opera while a son lies dying.

A desperate father paces the room. Every so often he goes to the phonograph that stands against the wall and restarts it.

He wishes it had struck him, let it take him, old, weak, widowed, alone. But his son, young and strong, is the one who has the Spanish flu, is the one who lies gasping, bleeding from the nose and ears, hot as a griddle to the touch.

His son owns a jewelry store in Chicago. He attends operas and polo matches, he has a wife and a daughter, he has done well, much better than his father. Still he comes back to Denver every year to visit. He came alone this time; his wife wouldn't travel with their daughter while the Spanish flu was rampant. He brought the phonograph along instead, as a gift. Entering his father's apartment, he looked around and smirked. "I knew you wouldn't have bought one for yourself."

With a rag daubed in a bucket of water, the father wipes his son, who lies naked on the bed. The apartment's two windows admit a cool November breeze, as well as the hullabaloo from the streets, but his son still sweats thickly. Small blood blisters have formed all across his pale skin.

His son set up the machine and showed him how to run it.

"Whose voice is that?" he'd asked his son.

"Jeanne Gerville-Reaché. I saw her once, onstage. My favorite contralto. A couple of years ago she died in her pregnancy."

"She's dead?"

"This was recorded shortly before she died. A beautiful lady."

Together they sat listening to the voice of a dead woman.

Now, in the street below, a brass band slowly passes, braying a version of *Oh! It's a Lovely War!*

His son had spent the last week sleeping on a cot under the window. When the father went out to work, his son visited old friends or went to see shows at a little theater that had stayed open despite the city's injunctions to combat the influenza. Evenings, the two of them sat drinking from bottles of wine that his son bought and listened to the phonograph, mostly to the contralto. At a certain point he realized that they were both longing for her, this woman whom he knew only by a voice, and who no longer lived.

He tries not to think of the telegram he will have to send to his daughter-in-law and granddaughter, tries to convince himself that, against all evidence, his son might still survive. Tries not to think of solitude. Of his wife who died many years ago, hacking with tuberculosis.

Toward the end of the recording, the singer's voice rises until she strikes against the limits of the machine's capabilities, and there it warbles strangely.

A raw fleshy scent fills the room. He wipes the blood from his son's face. In reality, he knows, all he is doing is all he can do: waiting for the end.

The contralto sings in a language that he doesn't understand, and he can't even guess what it is.

3. The Photo

"I wish it weren't already over," says the boy, sixteen. He looks around at the celebrants with dismay. He wears a pressed, new jacket that is too long for him and carries his hands in its front pockets.

"I guess you think you want to go to war." His father walks beside him, carrying a framed photograph.

"Yes!"

"I think I felt that way once, too."

The boy scowls and spits. He has been up, jittery with excitement, ever since the dark early-morning hours, when the newspaper companies began setting off a series of explosions to alert the city to the good news, and to sell their special editions. Now, a dozen hours later, the crowds on Sixteenth Street are still chanting, cheering, singing, beating pans, whistling, throwing confetti, waving flags. A car drags clattering pieces of stovepipe. A truck carries a pole with a hanging effigy of the Kaiser.

The boy tugs down his hat, which is also new, identical to the one that Harold Lloyd wore in *Two-Gun Gussie*. He stops to watch a young woman stroll by.

"Here," says his father, beckoning from a storefront: Mile High Photo.

Inside, in the quiet, the photographer fusses with his flash pan. "It will be better," he says, "with one of the backdrops. It will add some style."

The father looks at the photo in his hand. "No backdrop. Just a white wall."

The photographer shrugs, eager to move along. He's been busy all day.

"You kneel there," the father says. "I stand here."

"We can both stand," the boy says.

"No, the point is to make it just the same."

The boy, sighing, kneels. The father puts on his hat, and the boy does, too.

"No, no," the father says, "you hold yours on your knee."

"You're wearing yours."

"Yes, but yours goes on your knee."

"I'll wear it."

The father holds out the framed photo, making little sounds with his lips. "Look here—with my father, I had it on my knee. He wore his."

"Did Grandpa tell you to put it on your knee?"

"That's just how it turned out."

"I'll wear mine."

"When you have a son and you take this photo, you can wear the hat."

"I'd let my son wear his hat if he wanted."

"Sirs," the photographer says.

The father lets the boy wear the hat. "Wear it back, so the camera can see your eyes," he adds, to regain some authority. He sets aside the framed photo, and at the last moment he takes off his own hat, thinking there will be a symmetry in that. But after the flash shoots off—and briefly consumes the world with brilliant light—he begins to rue it.

They step outside into the moving crowds and come to Fifteenth Street before he realizes that he's forgotten his framed photo in the photographer's studio. He tells his son to wait while he goes back for it. When he reaches Fifteenth again, his son is smoking a cigarette—where did that come from?—and talking to a young woman in a long coat and a wide straw hat. She's pretty.

From behind her he gestures to his son and goes on alone. He walks looking at the framed photo of himself and his father in their old-fashioned clothes—frock coats and tall bowler hats. It's a photo of a man with a great silly grin standing just behind a boy on one knee, a boy who looks both desperately serious and thrilled just to be there, having his photo taken with his father.

4. The Leg

"Now Jack will soon be home."

Ralph has heard Mother say this twice already as she bustles around, bringing in cookies, then tea, and he has noticed that each time she says it, Father shifts his hands a little.

Ralph is sitting in the parlor of his father's Victorian house in the Highlands, in an ornate wooden armchair. His crutches are propped against the chair back. He gives two cookies to his son, who gravely and silently pockets them. To Ralph this seems strange behavior for a boy, but is it worrying or only amusing? He's not sure. When he returned from France two weeks ago—or, rather, when most of him returned, excepting the left knee, shin, and foot—his son screamed and cried at the sight of him. Ralph thought at first that it was because of the leg. But no, the boy simply had no idea who this man was.

"I wonder if he'll recognize Jack?" Mother says.

But Ralph has no doubt that the boy will. Jack—who could make coins appear out of noses, who could crawl around with his nephew for hours playing with tin soldiers—had been extremely popular.

Again Father's hands twitch.

Finally Mother stops moving, sits at the edge of a chair. She adjusts the plate of cookies and says, "Will you remember your Uncle Jack?"

The boy stares at her. He says, whispering, "Yes."

In the quiet afterward the noises of celebration carry to them. Church bells. School bells. Steam whistles.

Mother says to the boy, "I bet your mama is glad to have your daddy back to get you out of the house, so she can get a thing done."

The boy only stares.

Mother looks around the room, turns to the boy again. "Would you like to see if there's any dough left in the mixing bowl?"

The boy leaps from his seat, and so the two of them exit. Ralph feels inclined to run after them, but he remembers his leg, looks at his father, and sits still.

It'd been a surprise when Jack enlisted. He'd never expressed any interest before, but he'd gone to sign up while his arm was still in a sling, before the general conscription even began; he'd volunteered.

The sling resulted from a beating that Father gave Jack. Ralph had gone with Father in the Studebaker for an afternoon of fly-fishing, but Father had stepped on his rod and broke it, so they returned early; then, entering the house, they heard something strange upstairs and discovered Jack, naked, with another boy, also naked. Ralph had never seen the other boy before or again, only glimpsed him running past, wild blond hair, tanned, penis flapping.

When Ralph dragged Father away, he'd been afraid that Jack might already be dead.

"Do you suppose," Ralph says, "there's any chance at all that Jack could be home for Christmas?"

"When he left," Father says, "he told me that, one way or another, we would never see him again."

In the kitchen, the boy squeals and Mother laughs, the noise of them muffled by the door. Ralph pushes up to go to them, forgetting his leg, and falls.

5. The Dance

Is it the crowds or the crying baby? He contemplates the hysterical noises from the street of people shouting and smashing pans together, and he considers the urgent, remorseless vocal agony of the child. The problem is the baby. He could sleep through a celebration; it has nothing to do with him.

He needs sleep.

He grows angrier and angrier as insufferable minutes pass into an hour, and then another. He cannot sleep, and without sleep he will have no energy for his work. He might lose the job; others will be happy to do it. He cannot lose the job. And he cannot sleep. He cannot sleep because the baby won't be quiet. How can the baby continue like this? It seems inhuman. It seems pure malice, pure hatred, of him, the baby's father.

Finally he scrambles out of bed, throws the door open, and strides into the other room. His wife slouches in a kitchen chair with the baby in her lap, and he falls to a crouch before them and raises his fist over the shrieking creature.

His wife licks her lips. "Stop that," she says.

Her look catches him. "Can't I joke?" he says.

But she stares in a way that twists into him, and suddenly he understands that he will regret the gesture a long time. Already it makes him sad, to think of it, to think of thinking of it.

In repentance, he asks, "Is he sick?"

"It's the noise outside that keeps prodding him. Take him, please. He'll quiet for you. He always does."

He takes the baby to his shoulder. He paces and bounces his step. The trick involves adding movements within the movements, and he thinks of it as dancing very delicately. He has described it to his wife, but she isn't able to do it.

In a minute, the baby quiets.

A few minutes later, the baby curls and sleeps. Then his wife, too, sleeps in her chair.

He continues to circle the room, inhaling the baby's crude human scent. He can put him down—the baby would sleep on—but he keeps the baby on his shoulder.

New Hat
Connie Willis

1920s

New Hat

CONNIE WILLIS

"Sɪʀ, ʜᴏᴡ ʟᴏɴɢ ʙᴇғᴏʀᴇ ᴡᴇ ʀᴇᴀᴄʜ Dᴇɴᴠᴇʀ?" Cʟᴀʀᴀ ᴀsᴋᴇᴅ ᴛʜᴇ conductor timidly.

"Two hours, ma'am." *Good*, Clara thought, relieved. The lawyer would still be in his office. She could see him and find out what Uncle Matthew had left her in his will and maybe even catch a train back to Chicago tonight and not have to spend the night in Denver. If they even had a hotel. Kane had assured her Denver was a big city, but the towns the train had been passing through had grown smaller and smaller, and at several stops there hadn't been a town at all, just a dirt road leading off across the prairie. It looked exactly like the pictures of the Wild West she'd seen in books. "There won't be any Indians, will there?" she'd asked her fiancé.

"Of course not," Kane had said impatiently. "Cowboys and Indians were only in the old days. It's 1924. Denver's a modern metropolis now."

But there *were* cowboys. She'd seen them on their horses from the train window, and cowgirls, too. One had galloped alongside the train as if trying to outrun it, waving her broad-brimmed hat and grinning. And if there were still cowboys and cowgirls, there might be Apaches, too. "And I've never traveled anywhere alone, Kane," Clara'd said. "Can't you just write the lawyer and ask him to send the papers?"

"It'll take too long, sweetheart," he'd said. "Mr. Wolfson won't hold the offer open forever. If I want to get in on it, I need to do it now."

"But I don't know anything about wills. Couldn't you send your lawyer instead?"

"I need him here, and only you can sign the papers. And it's not as if you'll have to go the whole way alone. Aunt Pearl will be with you as far as St. Louis."

But his Aunt Pearl had been almost worse than going by herself. She'd talked the entire way about mashers and confidence men who preyed on young girls who traveled alone, undermining what little courage Clara had, and about how her daughter's fiancé would never have allowed her to go out to the Wild West by herself. "I mean, *anything* could happen to an innocent young girl in a place like that. Still, I suppose Kane knows what he's doing. And at least now you'll have an inheritance."

If Uncle Matt left me anything, Clara thought now. She'd tried to tell Kane she wasn't sure he'd had anything to leave, but he'd said, "He was a miner, wasn't he? He probably left you a gold mine. If he did, I'll let you buy a pretty new hat."

She looked around the train at the hats the other passengers were wearing. The prettiest one was a blue cloche that a girl who'd just gotten on was wearing. She was obviously traveling alone, too, though she didn't look nervous at all, not even when a man tried to sit down next to her. She calmly stood up and came over to sit across from Clara. "Safety in numbers," she said. "So, where are you going? Denver?"

Clara nodded.

"I'm going there, too, to teach school. I've been teaching in Yuma, but I decided I wanted to try life in the city."

"Alone?"

The girl laughed. "You sound just like Mother. She's convinced I'm going to be kidnapped by white slavers. She doesn't understand that women can take care of themselves nowadays. Are you going to Denver for a job, too?"

"No, I...have business there."

"Oh. I hope you get a chance to tour the West while you're here. There are all sorts of things to see, the Rockies and the Grand Canyon."

It's going to take all my courage just to make it to the lawyer's office and back home, Clara thought, and when they reached Denver she went straight to the taxi stand. "1438 Larimer Street," she told the driver.

He drove up a street lined with warehouses and then department stores. Ahead she could see a tall clock tower. Denver looked just like Chicago and not at all like the Wild West she'd imagined. There were trolley lines and streetlights and newsboys hawking the *Rocky Mountain News*, though she hadn't seen any mountains yet.

They turned onto Larimer Street, and there were the mountains, blue peaks off in the distance. They were beautiful. The buildings here were brick and not as tall or as fancy, mostly small shops, though she saw a hotel and several restaurants.

The taxi pulled over in front of a store that said "Tents." The one next to it said "Western Clothing," and next to that was a bicycle shop. "I don't think this is the right address," Clara said, but the taxi was already driving off. She picked up her suitcase and walked over to the western clothing store, looking for a number above the door, but there wasn't one, or on the tent store's awning. She walked back the other way, past a photographer's. Next to it was a restaurant with faded numbers painted above the open door. She went closer, peering up at them, and as she did, a huge cowboy appeared in the doorway. "Well, what do we have here?" he said, looming over her. He had a scruffy beard, and she realized to her horror that he had been drinking. It wasn't a restaurant at all. It was a speakeasy. Or a saloon! "You lookin' for me, girlie?"

"N-no," Clara stammered, backing away.

"Now, no need to go all skittish." He stepped down out of the doorway. "Come on in, and I'll buy you a lemonade." He reached for her arm.

"Tex! You stop that!" A tiny, apron-clad woman appeared in the doorway. "What do you think you're doin'?" She pushed her way between them. "You're scarin' her. Now, git!"

Amazingly, even though he was twice her size, the cowboy mumbled, "Sorry, ma'am," and shambled back inside.

"Don't mind him, hon," the woman said. "He don't get to town much. Now, how can I help? You lookin' for somebody?"

"Yes, 1438 Larimer Street."

"Two doors that way, where it says 'Western Clothing.'"

"Oh, but...," Clara said, dismayed, and fumbled in her bag for the lawyer's letter.

"Who exactly were you lookin' for, hon?"

"Mr. John Brewster. He's a lawyer."

"Oh, J. J.," she said, nodding. "His office is upstairs. The stairs are on the left."

"Oh, thank you," Clara said, hurrying back and up the stairs and knocking on a door with "John J. Brewster, Att'y-at-Law" on it.

"Come in," a female voice called, and she went in. A girl no older than Clara sat at a desk, typing. "May I help you?" she asked.

"Yes, thank you. I wish to see Mr. Brewster."

"He isn't in today. Would you care to make an appointment? Sometime next week?"

"Next week? Oh, but I've come all the way from Illinois—"

"Oh, golly, are you Miss Easton?" the girl said, jumping up. "We didn't expect you so soon. I'll go get him." She ran out, returning with a gray-haired man with a handlebar mustache. He was still pulling on his coat, and from the smell of spirits on his breath, he'd been at the saloon, too. *Oh, dear*, Clara thought.

"So you're Matt Easton's niece?" he said. "Glad t'meet you. Matt and I were up at Georgetown together in the silver mining days. Matter of fact, he left you shares in his mine."

A silver mine. Kane had been right.

"Not that they're worth anything. It played out years ago."

"Oh." Kane had told her to ask whether he'd held any stocks and bonds. She did.

"Nope." He led her into his office and over to his desk, which was littered with papers. He began shuffling through them. "Lucy, what in tarnation did you do with Matt's will?"

"I put it on your desk." She plucked it out of the mess, handed it to him, and said to Clara, "The papers aren't quite ready for you to look over. Mr. Brewster, why don't you have Miss Easton go back to her hotel and come in tomorrow morning?"

"I don't have a hotel yet," Clara said.

"Lucy, take her over to the Windsor and get her a room," Mr. Brewster said, "and then take her to the Manhattan and feed her some supper, while I—what did you do with that danged will?"

"I didn't do anything with it," Lucy said. "Here it is. And don't swear at me, you old coot, or I won't come back and help you." She turned to Clara. "I'll take you over to the hotel now," she said, and led her back along Larimer Street. "Sorry you caught us in such a muddle. We didn't think you'd be here till next week. But don't worry, it'll be fine tomorrow," and, when Clara shot her a doubtful glance, "I'll see to that. And you don't have to worry about Mr. Brewster. He likes a drink now and then, but he's honest as the day is long. I wouldn't work for him if he wasn't."

Clara believed her. She could envision her quitting if he did something she disapproved of, but that wasn't what was worrying her. She was worrying over how to tell Kane the bad news, so much so she didn't even taste her dinner, and as soon as she got back to the hotel, she told the clerk she needed to send a telegram. He handed her a yellow form and she printed, "KANE: NO STOCKS BONDS STOP MINE WORTHLESS CLARA," but then changed her mind. She needed to tell him herself, to explain, and to hear his comforting voice. She crumpled up the form and asked the clerk to put through a long-distance call to Kane for her.

"Have you seen the lawyer?" Kane demanded the moment she said hello. "What did your uncle leave you?"

"I don't know yet, but I'm afraid it wasn't much." She told him what Mr. Brewster had said about the mine and there not being any stocks and bonds. "He said Uncle Matt didn't—"

"What about railroad shares? Didn't he leave you *anything*?"

"I don't know. We haven't gone over the will yet."

"What have you been doing all this time? You know this deal can't wait."

"I know. I'm sorry," she said miserably.

"As soon as you know how much he left, let me know, but don't telephone. It's too expensive. Send me a telegram," he said and hung up. *Oh, please let Uncle Matt have had shares in* something, Clara thought. *And please let the papers be ready tomorrow.*

They were. The papers on Mr. Brewster's desk had been organized into tidy stacks, and a neat file labeled "Matthew Easton Estate" lay in the center of it. "We worked on it all night," Lucy whispered to her.

She'd tidied Mr. Brewster up, too. His hair and mustache were combed, his coat had been brushed, and he looked chastened. "Miss Easton, I'd like to apologize for yesterday. I'm afraid I was under the weather. Now, as to your uncle's will—"

"Did he have any railroad shares?"

"No, he thought they were too risky. He put all the proceeds of his mine into land."

"Land?" Clara said, thinking of the barren prairie she'd seen from the train window. It hadn't looked like it was worth anything, but maybe it would be enough for Kane's business deal. "How many acres?"

"Acres? I don't know. Maybe a dozen."

A dozen. Clara's heart sank.

"Lucy, where in tarnation's that list of the land—" he said, riffling through the papers. She handed it to him. "Your uncle left you five properties on Sixteenth Street here in Denver," Mr. Brewster read, "three on Fifteenth, four on Curtis, and five on Larimer Street, including the land this building sets on. Twenty-nine properties in all." He handed the paper to her. "Here's their assessed value and the annual income from them."

Clara stared at the totals. "But...I don't understand. I thought you said the mine was worthless."

"Now it is, but for a few years there it was a going concern, and land in Denver was dirt cheap back then."

It was more money than she'd ever imagined. Kane could buy into dozens of business deals with it. He wouldn't be angry with her, and Kane's Aunt Pearl couldn't call her a penniless orphan anymore.

"I imagine you'll want to talk this over with your fiancé before you make any decisions. If you want to telephone him, I can have Lucy put the call through for you."

"Thank you," she said gratefully, and as soon as Lucy told her he was on the line and shut the door behind her, "Kane, hello. I'm at the lawyer's office, and—"

"What are you doing phoning me? I told you to send a telegram. Do you know how much long distance costs?"

"Yes," she said, thinking, I hope Lucy isn't still on the line and hearing this, and then realized she couldn't be. If she were, she'd have spoken right up and defended her. "But, Kane—"

"This trip of yours has already cost me a fortune," Kane said. "Were there any railroad shares?"

"No," she said.

"I should have known better than to think anybody in your family would have had the sense to invest in anything," he said, but Clara wasn't listening. She was thinking about what Lucy would have said if Kane talked to her that way. Or the woman at the saloon. She had a sudden vision of her telling him, "Now, git!"

"And I should have known better than to send you out there, that it wasn't a job for a woman."

Clara thought of Lucy, who she was certain was responsible for every paper in that estate file, and of the teacher, and the cowgirl who'd raced the train.

"Tell Mr. Brewster that my lawyer and I will be handling the matter from now on," Kane said, "and catch the next train back. When you get here, I'll have you put the estate in my name. Do you understand?"

"Yes. Goodbye." She placed the receiver back on the hook and went to the door. "Mr. Brewster, can you arrange for me to draw against the estate for my current expenses?"

"Certainly."

"Good," Clara said. "I have some business to attend to, and then I want to take you and Lucy to lunch to celebrate."

"Of course. Lucy, would you accompany Miss Easton to her hotel?"

"No, I can find my own way. I'll meet you both at one o'clock at the Manhattan," Clara said and walked quickly back to her hotel and filled out a telegram form: "KANE STOP NOT COMING HOME STOP TOURING WEST INSTEAD CLARA." She handed it to the clerk.

"Are you sure that's what you want to send?" he asked. "That many words will be expensive."

"It will." She took the form back from him and added, "ALSO INTEND TO BUY A NEW HAT."

1940s

LENNIE'S TAVERN
SANDRA DALLAS

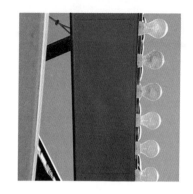

Lennie's Tavern

SANDRA DALLAS

Before the war, my brother and I hung out in the gin mills on upper Larimer Street, near the old Windsor Hotel. There was the Headquarters, the Lighthouse, the Easy Inn, and our favorite, Lennie's Tavern, which was next door to the Good Sisters Mission. Lennie's clientele was mostly retired railroad men who lived in the Roxbury Hotel or in the Barclay Rooms, and a few down-and-outers who slept in doorways or under the viaducts. For some reason, the pressmen from the *Rocky Mountain News* came all the way down to Lennie's after shift. That was when the *News* was in the old building on Seventeenth and Welton. The men wore overalls stained black with ink and those hats made from folded-up newspaper pages.

Larimer was seedy—and dangerous. It was said that any cat with a tail on Larimer Street was a stranger. It got worse while I was away, and so after the war, I didn't go down there. That was partly because I didn't want to get rolled, but it was mostly because Larimer brought back memories of my brother. I'd come back, but he hadn't.

One night, however, I was driving down Larimer and got to feeling nostalgic. So when I spotted a parking place at Nineteenth in front of Al Rudofsky's pawnshop, I decided to have a drink in the old place. It was January and cold. The snow stung my face like a hundred ice needles. The wind blew dried leaves down the gutter and wrapped a newspaper page around a light pole. I jammed my watch cap over my ears and pulled up my coat collar to keep my neck warm. A bum wearing one of those Eisenhower jackets that froze your ass off asked me for a quarter. He was shaking from the cold or maybe the DTs, and I thought he might be a vet, so I handed him a dollar and told him to go get warm. He must have followed me to Lennie's, because later I saw him there, passed out.

Lennie's hadn't changed. It still smelled of stale cigarette smoke and rancid grease, although I never saw anybody cook there—or eat there, either. The clientele hadn't changed. A cowboy wearing a big hat that was sweat-soaked at the creases sat with his feet on the table, his cracked boots held together with adhesive tape. Two railroad workers—you could tell by their striped jackets—smoked and played cards over their drinks. A couple of bums sat in the back, holding their beers as if they were afraid somebody would take them away. None of them looked up as I came in. Only one man sat at the bar, hunched over a drink and muttering. I sat down a stool away from him.

"What's yours, bub?" The bartender slid a dirty ashtray to me, although it hardly seemed necessary, since the bar was scarred black from snubbed-out cigarettes and others that had been left lying on the edge of the bar and had burned into the wood.

"Lennie still here?" I asked.

"I'm Leo. There ain't no Lennie." He was a wizened guy, dark, with a day's growth of beard. If he hadn't been standing behind the bar, I'd have thought he was one of the regulars.

"He was here back before the war. Lennie was."

Leo didn't care. He waited, so I ordered a beer and a shot, a boilermaker.

"Up in Butte they call that a Shawn O. You ever been to Butte?" The man on the stool didn't look up at me when he talked but stared at my beer glass. "That place is as cold in winter as the Hurtgen Forest."

"Neither place, Butte or Belgium."

Leo set down my boilermaker and rolled his eyes as if to warn me, but it was too late. I'd made the mistake of replying to the drunk, so he moved over onto the stool next to me and began talking about the war, Belgium mostly, and how cold it was. But I didn't mind. I had no need to tell strangers the details of what I'd been through. In fact, I wanted to bury the memories as deep as I could. But I knew some men had to talk it out. So I let him go on and didn't pay attention, only grunting now and then.

The bartender went to a jukebox and punched in something by the Andrews Sisters. The sisters weren't a big deal after the war,

but the records in the jukebox were old, might have been there the last time my brother and I were in Lennie's. Besides, you associated the Andrews Sisters with the war, so the music kind of went with the drunk's stories. I tapped my foot in time to the song, only half-listening to the man. Then he said, "You know what's the worst thing I ever saw?" I didn't reply, didn't want to hear what he'd seen, because I'd heard too many war stories already and experienced a few myself, but he continued anyway. "It wasn't anything the Germans did to us. It was what an American did to his buddy."

The drunk pointed to a bottle, the bartender poured a shot, and the man drank it down. "Why don't you give the guy a rest, let him drink in peace," Leo told him.

The drunk ignored him. "Man's inhumanity to man, that's what it was. Who said that?"

I shrugged. I didn't care. I wished he'd shut up now.

"You got a cigarette?" The man had black hair but a florid face and told me his name was Pinky. He lighted the Chesterfield I gave him, lighted it awkwardly, because he was missing the thumb of his right hand. He wedged the cigarette between his fingers, putting his entire hand over his mouth when he drew on the butt, then blew smoke at the pinup on a 1941 calendar behind the bar, covering her in a blue cloud. He waited until the smoke lifted, studying the woman as if he were some kind of art connoisseur. "We got captured, a bunch of us in the Hurtgen Forest, and we was so cold, not one damn one of us cared. We figured the Krauts'd put us out of our misery or else take us somewhere warm. Hell would have been okay." Pinky gave a snort of a laugh. "I guess that's what we got."

He hiked up the collar around his neck as if he were still cold and continued. "There was eight or ten of us, one wounded so bad he was out of his head. The Germans went off a little ways and talked to themselves. I didn't understand it, except for the word *juden*. We all heard it. There was a Jewish guy with us, a little pissant of a soldier, and he was scared. He said they were going to kill him because he had an *H* on his dog tags. *H* for Hebrew. That meant he was a kike." The drunk shook his head as if he were trying to shake away the memory. "So the son of a bitch grabbed the dog tags from the poor slob's neck and traded them for his own. When the Krauts checked the wounds, they saw that *H* and said *juden* again, and they shot him."

Pinky stared into his empty shot glass a moment and said, "Maybe he would have died anyway. Maybe they just put him out of his misery. What do you think?"

"War's hell, like they say," I mumbled. I turned away, and that's when I saw the bum I'd given the dollar to, lying across a table, his eyes closed. Under the Ike jacket, he wore an Army shirt and tie. Maybe he'd been an officer and had seen the kind of thing that Pinky had just described.

"That's not all," Pinky said. "The Jew went by the other man's name all the time he was a POW. You want to know what it was?"

"What's that?" I asked.

"Wiberstadt. Earl Van Antwerp Wiberstadt. Poor bastard had a chump name like that." The drunk started to laugh, and then he began crying, tears running down his face, his shoulders shaking. He put his head down on his arms and sobbed.

The story made me sick, and I stared at Pinky until the door opened, letting in the cold and the sound of an automobile horn out in the street. A woman in a dirty green coat with bleached hair, lipstick on her teeth, went over to the drunk. "Come on, honey. Let's get you something to eat. I got some cheese and crackers back in the room." She looked at me and said, "Somebody's got to take care of him."

"Leave him alone," I said, laying the pack of Chesterfields on the counter. She put a wad of chewing gum in the ashtray and removed a cigarette from the pack, then went over to the jukebox and found another Andrews Sisters song.

"He talks too much, even for a drunk," Leo said, looking at the cigarette package. When I nodded, he took one. "War's been over for a year." He lighted the cigarette, then poured me another shot. "On the house."

"He's the Jew, isn't he? The one who switched the tags."

The bartender shrugged. "Might be. I heard him tell that story a dozen times."

The man beside me stirred, and I told the bartender to pour him a shot. When the woman returned, sitting down on the stool with her knees wide, her elbows on the bar, Pinky said, "He's buying."

"Well, thanks," she said. "Give me a martini, Leo."

"You don't drink martinis." The bartender set down a glass of beer.

"How come you're buying?" she asked.

"I got a question to ask him."

Two men got up from a table, knocking over a glass and spilling beer. After they left, Leo went to the table to clean it up, and I realized the bar had emptied out. Even the bum I'd met on the street was gone.

"Earl Van Antwerp Wiberstadt," I said to the drunk. "That really his name, or did you hear it someplace?"

"It's real," the woman said. "Show him the dog tags. Show him." When Pinky didn't move, she reached into his coat pocket and pulled out a set of keys with the dog tags attached to it. "See. Dumbest name you ever heard, ain't it?" She threw the keys on the bar, got up, and said she was going to the little girls' room.

The man giggled. "It's his folks that ought to have died for hanging it on him, damn fool name." He looked at me, then at his empty glass. "How about another, mister, one for the road?"

I didn't buy Pinky another drink. I stared at the dog tags for a long time, opening and closing my right fist. Then suddenly, I grabbed Pinky by the lapels and yanked him to his feet. Pinky's eyes went big with fear, and I wondered if he'd looked at his German captors that way. "You son of a bitch!" I said. "That was my brother you killed. Earl Wiberstadt was my brother. You took his dog tags, so we never even knew what happened to him."

"I didn't kill nobody, mister. It wasn't me."

"Then how come you've got Earl's dog tags?"

The man tried to reply, but I had him around the throat. Leo had come up behind the bar, and he said, "I don't care what you do, but take it outside. I don't want to see nothing."

I dragged the man to the door. He was dead weight, and he didn't struggle, but I got him out of the bar all the same and shoved him up against a brick wall. I wanted to strangle him with my hands, but that was too quick. He started to protest, but I slugged him in the face, breaking his nose. Blood gushed onto his coat. The man put his hands in front of his face, and I gut-punched him. I slammed his head against the wall, and when he fell, I kicked him until he stopped moving. He didn't try to defend himself, and I thought maybe he wanted what he got. Maybe the beating would absolve him of a little guilt.

I should have left then, but I went back into the bar to pick up my coat. I wasn't worried that Leo would call the cops. He didn't care. And when the cops found the body, they'd think Pinky had been rolled, and they wouldn't care, either. I'd forgotten about the woman. She was back at the bar, smoking another one of my cigarettes.

"You kill him?" Leo asked, and I shrugged. I didn't know.

"What?" The woman gave me a sharp look.

"Your friend got what was coming to him," I told her. "He killed my brother."

"What are you talking about? He never killed nobody." She snubbed out the cigarette on the bar and dumped the lipstick-stained butt into the ashtray.

"He's the guy who switched the dog tags. They were my brother's. You think there's two guys in the US Army with that name?"

"You don't know nothing. He didn't switch any dog tags. He ain't even a Jew. A buddy of his give them to him. I seen it. The two of them was over there together."

"Sure," I said.

"Here, have another drink and shut up," Leo told her, handing her a bottle and a glass. "Take it over there." He pointed to the table.

"I won't shut up. You tell him, Leo. You tell him what happened."

I looked at Leo, who made a circle with his finger over his head to indicate that the woman was crazy.

"Don't you call me nuts," she said.

"Time for you to move along, honey," the bartender told her.

"I'll tell him then. I ain't moving till he knows. It was you, Leo. It was you give Pinky the dog tags. I seen you do it. You was the one switched them off that soldier. Pinky told me." She leaned back with a satisfied look on her face, and with the tip of her finger, she removed a speck of tobacco stuck to her lip.

The bartender didn't reply. He shoved the bottle toward me and said a second time, "On the house."

"Is that true?" I asked.

"He was almost dead, Earl was. He wouldn't have lasted an hour. They put him out of his misery is all. You wasn't there. You don't know how bad it was."

"I was there," I said. "I was on Bataan." I stared at Leo for a long time. Then I grabbed the bottle by the neck and, swinging it like a club, I smashed the bottles behind the bar, every damn one. Leo didn't try to stop me. Then I carefully took the dog tags off the key chain, put them into my pocket, and went out into the cold.

FENCE BUSTERS
MANUEL RAMOS

1950s

Fence Busters

MANUEL RAMOS

*who journeyed to Denver, who died in Denver, who came back
to Denver & waited in vain, who watched over Denver &
brooded & loned in Denver and finally went away to find
out the Time, & now Denver is lonesome for her heroes*

—Allen Ginsberg, *Howl*

KIKO TUGGED ON THE SHORT BRIM OF HIS CAP, A *CACHUCHA* TO
his mother, and adjusted the strap of his shoeshine box. Thick
black hair clumped around the edges of the cap. An October gust
streaked up Larimer Street. He squinted to block dust stirred from
the curb.

Kiko heard the announcer before he saw the radio. He felt the
speaker's excitement, but the boy didn't care much about the game.
The Dodgers weren't in it, again.

*Covington's sac fly to Mantle scores Mathews and ties the score at
three in the eighth inning. These pesky Milwaukee Braves won't give up.*

He slipped the card out of his shirt pocket and looked at it for
the hundredth time that day. Rival Fence Busters. Willie Mays wore
a magnificent smile as he admired Duke Snider's muscular right arm.
His father said it wasn't much of a tip. Kiko disagreed. It might have
been his best tip ever.

Kiko nodded at the man sprawled in the entrance to El
Charrito. A torn and stained overcoat partially covered the wino's
dusty pants and shirt. Kiko's mother called the bums *desgraciados*,
but his father said that word was mighty fancy for men who lived
on skid row.

Hank won't be there long, Kiko thought. He peered into the
cafe and breathed the familiar smells of roasted chile, fried beans,
and warm tortillas, but it was a mistake to allow the smells to
linger. He had at least three hours before he returned to his home,
and supper.

"Hey, Shiner," Hank murmured. "Spare a dime? I could use a cup a coffee."

"*No hablo inglés*," Kiko lied.

"Come on. You know me. I helped your old man move all that junk into your house. Don't give me that no in-gless stuff. You speak English good as me. For a Mex."

"I need lunch money. Why do you think I'm out here on Wednesday? You better move. Here comes Wanda."

The waitress gripped a broom as she marched to the doorway. The men listening to the game cheered her on.

"Get 'em, Wanda! *¡Ándale!* Throw 'em out!"

"Avay from 'yer! Ya' stinkin' up da place!" Her jowls jiggled and sweat dotted the white skin above her bright red lips.

Kiko smiled. Her words sounded funnier than a regular *gabacha*, another word from his mother. When Kiko mentioned her, his sister Elena said that the waitress was Polish and Kiko had to ask his teacher what that meant.

He tipped his cap, as his father had taught him. Wanda winked. She slammed the broom across Hank's legs and a cloud of dried mud and stale wine exploded.

Kiko headed for the new restaurant, just opened by the Silvas fresh from Chihuahua. The place might have men who needed clean shoes for the weekend, who had twenty-five cents for the brightest shine in Denver, and who wouldn't joke about Mexicans.

He waited for traffic to thin out and then crossed Twenty-first, in the direction of the downtown skyscrapers and construction projects. Mariachi music seeped through the walls of the American Inn. Kiko recognized the tune, something his mother listened to. He thought about going inside, but reconsidered. Too early for dance hall men.

He sauntered past the glass panes of Johnnie's Market and avoided the wide-eyed stare of the hairless goat head perched next to jars of pickled pigs' feet, bags of *ojas* for tamales, ristras of dark chiles, sacks of beans.

Kiko stopped at the Monterey House. He smelled fresh paint. A sign in the window said "Open," but something was wrong. A few adults and several children gathered in the middle of the large room, but there was no food and no one looked like a customer.

He inched into the doorway. The oldest man shook his head as he rocked on his boot heels and his chair's back legs. "No lights," he said. "Maybe next week." The man turned to a woman standing behind him. "I didn't know about no deposit for Public Service. How was I to know?" he asked in Spanish.

Kiko trekked on. He hadn't made any money all afternoon. His father often teased him about the lack of income from his shoe-shining job. "You spend hours *en las calles*, and you come back with maybe *cincuenta centavos*? Less than a dollar? *¿Como?* How does that happen? There are hundreds of men in this city who need clean shoes. Businessmen, bankers, *abogados*. All you got to do is ask, *mi'jo*. Just ask. That's how it is in this country. Do something for them, and they have the money to pay. *A eso le dicen la oportunidad.*"

Opportunity. Kiko had his doubts. He switched the strap again and rubbed his shoulder. His mother would want to massage him with *osha*. His arms were tired, his feet hot and grimy, and his cap too tight. He walked for several minutes without realizing where he was going. He ambled to a stop, like a car out of gas. The sign over his head announced "Cantina."

Bar. Café. El Chapultepec. He walked in.

Baseball played in the background.

What a finish! Adcock scores on Bruton's single in the tenth and the Braves win Game One of the 1958 World Series. Another outstanding performance by Spahn—he went the distance.

Stools rested against the bar and booths hugged the wall. Kiko only glanced at the large mirror behind the bar but he had an impression of decorated boats, flowers floating on water, and men in large straw hats.

Two men sat in a booth, drinking beer and smoking cigarettes. They stared at the boy. Kiko thought he saw one of the men spit on the floor under their table. Another man leaned on the bar, half-on and half-off a stool.

"The Braves? Give me a break," the man on the stool said.

The bartender poured whisky into the man's glass. "Where's your Red Sox, Jack? When's the last time they were in the Series?"

Jack groaned.

Kiko took a deep breath.

"Shoeshine? Only a quarter for the best shine in Denver."

Jack looked down at Kiko. The bartender said, "Leave my customers alone…," but Jack raised his hand and the bartender shrugged. Jack wore a wrinkled blue shirt, a cap that looked like Kiko's, except more ragged, and cracked brown loafers. Not the signs of a man who cared about the luster of his shoes. Kiko turned to leave.

"Why not?"

"You sure, Jack?" the bartender asked.

"Yeah, Jimmy. It's all right. The last time I got a shine was in Denver. Seems like a karmic thing to do." He sat on the edge of a booth.

Kiko knelt on the floor and opened his box, exposing rags, brushes, and a foot rest carved by his father. He took out a tin of shoe wax. Jack lifted his right shoe to the foot rest.

Kiko concentrated on his work. "What's your name, kid?" Jack asked.

"Francisco, but everyone calls me Kiko. Some are calling me Shiner."

"Shiner? I like that. It could mean different things. Words are like that. Different meanings depending on the talker so in the end they don't mean anything at all."

Jack took off his cap and his hair lay smashed against his forehead. His eyes were ringed with dark, puffy skin.

"If you say so, mister."

"Yeah. If I say so. You from here, Shiner?"

"Curtis Street. Over a few blocks."

"I know where Curtis is. We watched baseball near there, on Welton. Years ago. Good crowds back then. Those kids were serious about their ball playing. Whites and Negroes; Mexicans, Indians. All kinds. In team uniforms. That was cool."

Kiko wasn't sure if he should respond. "I guess," he said.

"I used to live here. My best friend is from here. We had good and bad times in this town, but they were all good when you think of it." He paused. "What I meant was, you born here? In the States?"

Kiko flinched. He had heard this kind of talk before. His parents spoke to him about being a citizen of the United States, no matter what anyone said. He had every damn right to be here. That's how his father put it.

"Yeah."

"That's good. Something to be proud of. Born into the mystery of this country, and the dream. Just don't let them get you down."

Kiko's customers had said many strange things while he popped his rags over their shoes. His father had told him to ignore the strangeness: "I don't understand these people. That's up to you to figure out, *mi'jo*. Until then, do the job and get paid."

Kiko bent closer to the shoe to rub extra hard on the thin leather. The baseball card slid out of his pocket.

"What's that?" Jack asked.

Kiko picked up the card by the tip of a corner and handed it to Jack. He hoped he hadn't smudged it.

"This is great. I saw these two play when they were in New York."

"You did? In person? Playing baseball?"

Jack laughed. "Sure, kid. I watched Mays and Snider go head-to-head, a couple of times. Mays was like an antelope in the out-field, maybe a jaguar, but I never saw a jaguar, so I can't say for sure. And Snider? Flatbush royalty. But I was at Yankee Stadium when the Red Sox were in town."

Kiko finished the shoe. He stretched. Jack returned the card.

"You ever talk with them?" Kiko asked.

"Shiner, you wouldn't believe. I've been at parties with guys like this. I signed a book for the Duke. And he autographed a ball for me."

"The kid don't know what you're talkin' about," Jimmy said. "Jack's a writer. Kind of famous these days because of his book from last year. There's no livin' with him now. I remember when he was just another barfly, him and his crazy pals. Bunch of goofs and drunks and so-called poets. Jack put them in his stories and now he's the toast of the upper crust. Goes to show."

"Come on, Jimmy. Don't you give me a hard time, too."

Jimmy turned off the small television set. He walked around the bar to the jukebox. He pressed a switch and the box came to life with running streams of light and a soft hum. A tube of blue light surrounded the gold and red machine like a halo. Jimmy punched a few buttons and music played.

"Blakey and Monk," Jack mumbled. "Johnnie Griffin. Nice." His head bounced to saxophone and piano riffs.

Kiko decided he liked the music. He was almost done with Jack's shoes.

"Whatever happened to that friend of yours?" Jimmy asked. "That car-thievin' wild kid? I ain't seen him for years."

Jack lit a cigarette. "Let me get my drink, Shiner." He stood up, walked over to the bar, and lifted his glass. He finished what was left of the whisky and coughed.

"Neal's in California."

"That right?" Jimmy responded. "What's he gonna do there he can't do here? Too many people on the Coast already. Denver's just right for me."

"He wants to leave. Always on the move, running from something. But he's stuck now."

"Why's that?"

"He checked into the Hotel San Quentin. Got a lease for something like ten years."

"Who'd he kill? The pope?"

"Just tried to be free in the land of the free, but now he knows that freedom is a crime, and it's sure not free. Or something like that." His words cracked with a half-laugh, half-sigh. He sat back down.

"He should'a never left Denver," Jimmy said.

"We all leave some day. Neal can't stop leaving. I worry that he's anchored for years. It could kill him." He inhaled smoke and then tapped his cigarette in an ashtray that looked like a Mexican sombrero. "I made the book people pay for a trip to Denver. They got me everywhere else selling books that haven't been written. I thought I owed it to Neal, but now I don't know why I'm here. It's not the same."

Kiko replaced the cap on the tin and tossed it into the box. He folded his buffing rag, placed it in the box, wiped his hands on another rag, and shut his box.

Jack admired his shoes. The cracks were still visible and the worn heels would never be replaced but the leather gleamed like clean rain on a new highway.

"That should impress the Hollywood wolves waiting to tear me apart." He pulled a crunched dollar bill from his pants pocket. "Keep the change."

Kiko touched his cap with his fingertips. "Thanks, mister. Much appreciated."

"Send that greaser over here. I could use a shine, but I ain't payin' no buck. Maybe a dime, if he's any good."

One of the men sitting at the booth pointed at his shoes. His drinking partner grunted a laugh.

"Sorry, mister. It's a quarter for a shine," Kiko said.

"Just get your brown ass over here."

"It's a quarter, mister."

"Shine my shoes and you'll get what you get, which might be a whippin' if I don't like the job you do."

The friend grunted again. A toothy grin creased his face and his eyes lit up in expectation. "You tell him, Leonard."

"Hey, knock it off," Jimmy said. "No call for that."

"Mind your business. I don't like dirty Mexicans hanging around when I drink my beer. And I really don't like the ones who talk back." Leonard chugged his drink. "I had my doubts about this place, just from the spic name. I told you that, didn't I, Tom?" Tom nodded eagerly. "You don't run a respectable joint," Leonard continued. "You let in those kind."

"Get out!" Jimmy shouted.

The two men stood up. Leonard grabbed Kiko's shoulder and squeezed. The boy tripped over his box and fell. His cap rolled down his back.

Jack jumped to his feet. "You're tough with a kid. Try someone your own size." Leonard threw a punch that missed. Jack grabbed Leonard's shirt collar with his left hand and swung his right fist into Leonard's jaw. Kiko heard a loud crack. Leonard dropped to his knees. Tom moved to jump on Jack but Jimmy had rushed from behind the bar. He held a baseball bat.

"Scram! Take this piece of crap with you," Jimmy said.

Tom picked up Leonard by the armpits and pushed him through the door. Leonard cupped his jaw. Tom hollered ugly curses but the two men did not look back.

A man in a suit walked in. "What's going on here? That man looked hurt. Another fight? You drunk again?"

Jack's laugh drowned the jukebox. "Not yet, Perry. But very soon, that's a promise."

Perry grabbed Jack by the elbow and started to guide him out. "We're almost late for the college. I can't leave you for a half hour without some disaster happening. Come on, let's go."

Jack twisted free. He stacked dollar bills on the bar. "Thanks, Jimmy. Next time."

Jimmy shook Jack's hand. "Any time."

"Take care of yourself, Shiner. Like I said, don't let the sons of bitches get you down."

Jack and Perry left. They climbed into the back of a black automobile and drove away.

Kiko waited on the sidewalk. The skyline stretched against the powder blue sky. He thought he could touch the buildings from where he stood. Cars and buses roared through the streets. Construction crews climbed steel skeletons; cement mixers, trucks, and cranes shrieked into the pure air. Hobos stood in line for hours, dancing to sirens and cop whistles. Stray dogs barked at baseball players in the park on Welton; a color television set turned on for the first time in a large house on the edge of the city; the newsman talked about the upcoming Sputnik first anniversary. Irish songs and Italian mandolins mixed with the smells of fresh tamales and boiled chitlins. Church bells, synagogue chants, and Arapaho drums echoed along the Valley Highway.

Sometimes words don't mean anything at all.

Kiko hung the strap on his shoulder, lifted his box, and walked into Denver's heart.

"I'll have to read Jack's book," he said to Duke and Willy.

The Welcome
Arnold Grossman

1960s

The Welcome

ARNOLD GROSSMAN

"WHAT ARE YOU, A COWBOY OR A QUEER?"

It was a deep, resonant voice, laced with whiskey and cigarettes, that startled Zack Blum, sending a bolt of fear surging through his body.

He made no attempt to drop the newspaper he had been reading. Instead he stole a glance down at the tan granite floor and saw a pair of scuffed, steel-tipped cowboy boots pointing at him.

"I said, what are you?" The voice was louder now, more challenging. Zack had no choice but to lower the paper enough to take in a towering figure of a man dressed in worn bluejeans with a large brass buckle, plaid shirt, and a cowboy hat that added a good six inches to his height. His face looked as if it had been sculpted from saddle leather, and his piercing, gray eyes, barely visible through squinted lids, looked as cold as the air felt in the deserted terminal.

"Sorry, were you talking to me?"

"I don't see anyone else here wearing boots like a cowboy and long hair like a girl, do you?"

"Guess not," were the only words Zack could muster, his eyes searching the empty waiting room, hoping for someone else to appear. But there was no one. He tried to see if the lone ticket agent he had noticed earlier was still at his window, but he was not, although a light remained on. The Continental Restaurant, with its Caboose Bar, where he had seen a family of four finishing their meal, had closed its doors. Zack suddenly felt very much alone.

"I'm waitin'," demanded the man, who continued glaring down at Zack.

"Neither."

"Neither? You don't know what you are?"

"I'm not a queer," Zack finally said, feeling his shoulders tense up as if they could protect him from the sudden blow he feared was soon to come his way.

"If you're not no queer, maybe you're a damn hippie. Which is just as bad, don't you think, Nathan?"

"You got that right." It was another deep whiskey voice, this time coming from behind. Zack could not resist turning to look over the high back of the yellow oak bench he remained glued to, to see another big man, also a cowboy with a tall hat and a weathered face, but wearing a broad grin.

Zack felt a momentary sense of relief when he heard the scraping of metal wheels on stone and saw a black man, wearing a red porter's hat and pushing a green wooden baggage cart past the ticket windows. Zack saw his skis and duffle bag on the cart.

"Excuse me, I need to get my stuff. On that cart."

The cowboy in front of him turned to look over his shoulder and called out to the porter, "You can drop this guy's stuff there on the floor, boy."

The porter, whose gray hair beneath the red cap and slow gait said he was at least in his sixties, shook his head and let his shoulders sink in resignation at what he had just been called, as though it wasn't the first time. He stopped the cart and summarily dropped the skis and duffle on the floor and continued on his way, disappearing through a door marked "Baggage."

Now the man named Nathan moved around the end of the bench and stood beside the first cowboy. The two were so close that Zack could smell alcohol and fried food on their breaths, and something like a barnyard on their clothes.

It was far from what Zack had expected in the way of a welcome to Colorado, where he was about to begin graduate school at the University of Colorado in nearby Boulder. What he had expected was to see his friend and fellow New Yorker, Dutch, who had agreed to pick him up after he returned from skiing. But Dutch had not yet shown up. Now faced with the two cowboys, Zack thought of making a break for the newsstand at the far end of the waiting rooms, where lights still burned, and where the elderly manager had been friendly to him.

"Come off the silver lady, did you?" the man had asked.

"Sorry?"

"The California Zephyr. That's what they call her, I guess because she's so elegant. And fast, too."

Zack said yes, he had arrived on the Zephyr from Chicago and that his trip had begun in New York. He'd bought a copy of the *Rocky Mountain News* to help pass the time while he waited for his friend to arrive.

"It's ten cents," the man had said when Zack dropped a nickel on the counter. Zack had pointed to the five-cent price at the top of the front page, and the man had added, "It's for overhead. Not sure what that is, except maybe my salary. Some overhead."

The man had asked if Zack was a baseball fan, like most New Yorkers. Zack had nodded. Had he ever seen Willie Mays play in the old Polo Grounds? He had, several times with his father, who later would never forgive the Giants for abandoning New York for San Francisco. The man then had shared some of his own memories of Mays, surprisingly reciting the famous outfielder's lifetime batting average, the longest ball he ever hit—560 feet into the center-field bleachers, off the Dodgers' Ralph Branca—and what his favorite pitches were, all of which duly impressed Zack.

As Zack pondered what fate awaited him at the hands of the two men confronting him, he buttoned up the collar of his olive drab Army surplus field jacket, which did little to protect him from the frigid winter air that had seeped into the terminal. Beneath the jacket was a heavy tweed turtleneck sweater, over which his long black hair spilled down to his shoulders. The cowboy boots he wore were a going-away gift from his girlfriend, who had told him they'd be appropriate for Colorado. But they did very little to protect his feet from the biting chill.

Now, as he looked up at the two men who were bent on making things miserable for him on his first night in Colorado, he asked himself, Why him? Maybe it was the cowboy boots, which they seemed to think someone with long black hair didn't deserve to wear. He only knew they did not like the looks of him, any more than they seemed to like the looks of the old porter. He wished Dutch would soon come through the heavy doors from the street, or, better still, a cop.

"That today's paper?" demanded the first cowboy.

Zack nodded, reading in a shaky voice that he wished he could force lower, "Saturday, January 14th, 1961." He also saw a headline that read, "Stock Show Brings Usual Sub-Zero Weather to Town."

"I don't imagine you're in town for the National Western, now are you?"

"What's that?"

Nathan laughed. Actually, it was more of an equine snort, which seemed fitting enough.

"You smartin' off with us?" asked the first man.

"No, I'm new in town. I don't know names of places."

"It ain't a place. It's the stock show. The National Western Stock Show. With the biggest rodeo in the West. You never heard of it?"

"Sorry, no, I haven't."

"Where you from, anyway?" asked the nameless cowboy.

"A lot of places."

"Know what I think? I think you're from New York, that's what."

"Nooooo York?" echoed Nathan in mock surprise.

"Lemme see that," said the first cowboy, grabbing the newspaper from Zack's hands.

The man leafed through the first few pages and studied one of them, nodding, and handed the paper back to Zack.

"What does that say, Mister, or Miss, New York?" His grimy index finger pointed to a bold headline above a picture of a young man with a shaved head.

Zack stared at the words, wishing he could make them disappear. Then he read softly, "Long Hairs Become Targets of Stock Show Cowboys With Sheep Shears."

Nathan let out another snorting laugh. His partner grinned, a menacing grin, and took a pair of chromed manual hair clippers from a back pocket, squeezing the handles opened and closed.

"That's us," he said.

"Like the paper says, we're the cowboys with sheep shears," added Nathan.

Zack decided to make his move. He sucked in a deep breath, dropped the newspaper, and tried to get up, but the cowboys stood their ground, and he bumped into the first one's chest and fell back down on the bench.

The silence of the large room was broken by an amplified voice echoing off the stone walls. "Announcing the last boarding call for the Colorado Zephyr, to San Francisco, California, with stops at Salt Lake City and Reno, Nevada, departing on Track 3, down the ramp at the north end of the terminal. Welcome aboard."

The two cowboys were distracted by the announcement and looked around the waiting room. There was a commotion behind them, several sets of footsteps. Zack turned, along with the two cowboys, to see the family that had been dining in the restaurant. They hurried across the waiting room toward the tunnel. The woman's high heels beat a rapid rhythm on the granite. She held the hands of a young boy and girl, who tried to keep up with her. The father, now wearing a gray fedora and holding a suitcase in each hand, glanced back, frowning. Zack realized the man was staring at him, not at the cowboys.

"Let's make it snappy," said the father to his family, "or we won't be going to California tonight."

After the travelers disappeared down the ramp, the cowboys turned back to face Zack again.

"Wouldn't you like to be on that train, too, hippie? But you ain't goin' nowhere," said the cowboy with the shears.

Zack said nothing, but only looked longingly at the tunnel entrance.

Still squeezing the shears open and closed, the big cowboy grabbed a handful of Zack's hair and pulled it taut. Reacting to the pain, Zack instinctively reached up and grabbed the wrist of the cowboy, who only yanked his hair harder. "Hold still, queer-boy, or I'll cut off more than your damn hair."

"I didn't do anything to you. Why don't you just leave me alone?" said Zack, his fear giving way to anger.

"We'll leave you alone once we give you your new haircut. Maybe."

"You didn't hear him. He said leave him alone." Both cowboys jerked their heads to see the balding man from the newsstand standing at the end of the bench, his voice devoid of the friendliness Zack had heard earlier. His nostrils were flared, his eyes narrowed. And he held a baseball bat in one hand.

"Don't be lookin' for trouble, old man," said the cowboy still holding Zack's hair.

"I'm not. And I'm thinking you shouldn't be, either, 'less you want to feel some hickory upside your head."

The cowboy let go of the hank of hair and, holding the shears in his hand like a weapon, advanced on the newsstand man, who stood his ground, moving the ball bat ever so slightly up and down.

"Put that thing down, before you get hurt," said the cowboy, lunging.

In a blur of movement, the bat came up and then down, squarely on the hand that held the shears, which flew out of the cowboy's hand and skittered loudly across the floor. The cowboy doubled over in pain, squeezing his hand between his knees.

"You busted my damn hand, you crazy bastard."

Nathan took a step toward the old man. The bat came up in the air as the man holding it poised to bring it crashing down again, this time on a skull.

Nathan raised his hands and shook his head. "Ease off with that bat, mister."

"Not until you and your pal get on out of here."

Nathan slowly took two steps back, not taking his eyes off the poised bat, stopped for a moment, then moved farther back.

"You okay?" Nathan asked his partner, who shook his head.

"Hell no, I'm not."

"There's a drugstore a few blocks from here, past Larimer Street," said the man with the bat. "They could probably fix you up with something for the pain. They're open late. You'd be well advised to get on up there."

The two cowboys stood speechless, exchanging wary glances. They finally turned and moved toward the terminal doors that led outside to Wynkoop Street. The man from the newsstand watched them. So did Zack. When the doors closed behind the cowboys, Zack turned to the man, who nodded.

"You all right, son?" he asked.

"I guess so."

"You'll stop shaking soon."

"You really know how to swing that bat."

"Not quite like Willie Mays did. But there weren't ever many who could."

"I want to thank you for what you did."

"No need to. They're just trash, out lookin' for trouble. I'm sure you've got some back in New York, too." Zack nodded, smiling. He held out his hand, which the man took in a firm grip. "I'm glad I met you. Really glad. My name's Zack. Zack Blum."

"Likewise. I'm Jimmy Holmgren."

Zack looked at the bat again and noticed, for the first time, the name burned into the wood near the wide end: Jimmy Holmgren.

Zack wondered about the bat, about the name on it.

But then he was distracted by a familiar voice.

"Hey, Zack. Man, I'm sorry I'm late. Traffic was a bitch."

Dutch stood there in his ski clothes, his face bright red from a day on the slopes.

"No big deal."

"We were just passing the time," said Jimmy Holmgren to Dutch as he turned and shuffled toward the newsstand. He called over his shoulder to Zack, "You might want to set that Bulova back an hour, son. It's Mountain Standard Time out here."

Zack watched the old man disappear, then picked up his skis and bag and followed his friend out into the night. The air was cold enough to turn their breaths to steam. "You ever hear of a ballplayer named Jimmy Holmgren?" Zack asked.

"Sure. Why?"

"That was him, the old guy. He just about saved my life."

"You serious?"

"Yeah, I am. Who was he?"

"He played in the majors way back in the twenties, just one season, for the Reds. Hit five hundred. Then he got kicked out of baseball for cracking a guy's skull with a bat. Haven't you heard of him?"

Zack shook his head.

"Maybe he's not that memorable," said Dutch.

"He is now."

Something in Common
Robert Greer

1970s

Something
in Common

ROBERT GREER

THE MID-OCTOBER MILE HIGH CITY AIR WAS DRY, CRISP, AND rich with the home-again smell of burning leaves and the barest hint of ponderosa pine. It was a scent that temporarily served to suppress the lingering smell of napalm, machine-gun oil, and jungle rot that CJ Floyd had lived with for the past two years. Hours earlier, after rising from another sleepless night, the decorated Vietnam veteran had decided to retrieve something he'd left behind before going off to war. Something from the past that he hoped would help him build a bridge to the future and outrun his demons.

Two months earlier he'd returned home to Denver after serving back-to-back one-year tours of duty as an aft-deck machine gunner on a 125-foot Navy patrol boat in Vietnam. Like so many of his generation, he'd seen far too much of the dark side of the world, even though he was barely twenty years old. He'd killed people and watched people being killed. He'd had time to think about what it would be like to die. He'd eaten more C-rations than he cared to remember, and more than once, in the middle of some humid Mekong Delta estuary, he'd washed the US Navy's canned mystery-meat delicacy down with swamp mushrooms and roasted river rat.

While on R&R in Saigon, he'd made love to delicate, beautiful, war-numbed women for less than the cost of a car wash in the States, often wondering as he did if he would be the GI to finally crush what remained of his paid lover's spirit. He'd thrown up at the horror that was war—often—and every day while he was in-country he'd prayed that he'd make it home. Now at least the physical side of his ordeal was behind him. There'd be no more search-and-destroy missions. For the moment he was on a mission of retrieval.

As he stepped off the No. 15 RTD bus at the intersection of Colfax and Larimer streets to head for GI Joe's, a Larimer Street pawnshop, he took a long, deep breath. The word *home* briefly crossed his mind. Smiling a nervous smile, he teased a cheroot out of the soft pack he'd extracted from the left pocket of his peacoat and toyed with the miniature cigar. He hadn't been a smoker when he'd left for Vietnam in 1969. Now he was. He slipped the cheroot loosely between his lips and wondered whether the antique license plate he'd pilfered from a GI Joe's display case two years earlier and hidden behind three loose wall tiles at the groutless seam of an electrical box three days before he shipped out for Vietnam would still be there.

He couldn't be certain that the skid row pawnshop would even still be standing, because many Larimer Street buildings and dozens of neighboring structures for blocks around had been bulldozed as part of Denver's ongoing Skyline Urban Renewal Project while he'd been gone. But if the pawnshop was there, he had the eerie feeling that the antique porcelain license plate would still be there in its place as well. There to soothe his psyche and offer him a belated welcome home.

It's often been said that you can tell a lot about a man by what he reads, and there's probably substantial truth to that. But you could learn much more about a man like CJ Floyd by taking a long, hard look at the things he had little use for and the things he'd saved. CJ saved ticket stubs from plays and movies and every manner of game. His collectibles included a ticket stub from the Denver Rockets' inaugural ABA basketball game. He had two unused tickets to the 1969 Denver premiere of *Butch Cassidy and the Sundance Kid*. He'd won those tickets by being the tenth caller to a local radio sports talk show and had never used them because three days before the movie's opening, and ten days before shipping out for Vietnam, he'd come down with a case of the flu that had kept him bedridden for a week.

The earthen quarter-basement of the Victorian home where he'd been raised by his alcoholic bail-bondsman uncle on Denver's Bondsman's Row was cluttered with coffee cans full of cat's-eye marbles, jumbos, and hundreds of rare and valuable steelies, too. Stacks of mint-condition 45s and unopened LPs stored in dusty

plastic-covered tomato crates filled every corner of the musty underground room.

During his teenage years, CJ had been a gangly, standoffish, out-of-place, six-foot-two black kid with a massive Afro, seemingly nowhere to go, and a sad, lost look on his face all too often. He'd spent most of his free time during those years checking out garage sales, estate liquidations, and antique auctions. A collector in the old-fashioned sense, CJ saw himself as a guardian of the precious things from other eras. For him, everything he collected represented an important trail to the things he wanted to remember from his own past. Conspicuously missing from his collectibles were report cards and family-oriented board games, the follow-the-leader, all-too-human possessions that required interacting with other people instead of going it alone. For CJ, there were no albums filled with Pop Warner football pictures or photographs of grade-school field trips to the art museum. No yearbooks or kindergarten "mommy and daddy" paintings. No mementos from debutante balls or forgotten souvenirs from the prom. CJ's collectibles were the treasures of a loner, artifacts assembled by someone who'd spent a lifetime running against the wind.

CJ's collection of antique license plates, a collector's equivalent of Olympic gold, said more about him than any of his other collections. He'd begun the collection during his early teens, when his Uncle Ike's drinking had reached its peak and street rods and lowriders had taken the place of family in CJ's life.

The pride of his collection were his 1917 New Hampshire plate and his prized 1919 Denver municipal tag. Both had been fabricated using the long-abandoned process of overlaying porcelain onto iron. Although his collection was impressive, it remained incomplete, and Ike, one of the few people who had ever seen the entire collection, suspected that like CJ, fatherless and abandoned by his mother before he could walk, it would remain forever less than whole.

Most of the buildings in the 2100 block of Larimer Street, including GI Joe's, had escaped demolition during CJ's absence, but scores of buildings to the east and west had been leveled, leaving a barren, war-torn-looking landscape in their wake.

GI Joe's shared a white two-story brick building that had been erected in 1893 with Lucero's Furniture Store. The second-floor windows of the pawnshop had been bricked in and painted white, giving the building the neo-Gothic look of a mortuary. Joe Rubinson, a returning World War II veteran, had established the business in the late 1940s, and the shop, along with its next-door pawnshop neighbor, Pasternack's, had a reputation for selling everything from college scholastic honorary keys to microscopes for University of Colorado medical students.

Wiley Ames, a World War II veteran, onetime alcoholic, former Denver skid row derelict and Salvation Army reclamation project, had helped manage GI Joe's for nearly two decades. His left arm, a casualty of the war, was a ten-inch-long amputation stump. Over the decades, Wiley had exorcized his war demons, and now, at the age of forty-six, he was a teetotaling, psychologically whole fitness devotee. He had a street reputation as a no-nonsense straight shooter with a soft spot for hard-luck stories.

The wind kicked up out of nowhere as CJ Floyd entered GI Joe's. Uncertain exactly how to proceed with his mission of retrieval, he stood inside the entryway of the dimly lit establishment, waiting for his eyes to accommodate to what could best be described as a life-size rectangular box of clutter.

Moving purposefully into the musty bowels of the store, past glass-topped display cabinets and row after row of shelves chock-full of everything from slide guitars to roller skates, he had the sense that he was back in the Mekong River Delta, cruising through enemy territory well beyond the safety of the 42nd River Patrol Group's operations base and home.

His heart sank when he stopped to glance across the room toward his remembered landmarks—the electrical box and a bank of loose tiles. Feeling defeated and surprisingly a little cheated, he took a hesitant step in the direction of what was no longer a wall of failing tile and cracking plaster but instead a whitewashed area filled with art, and he sighed.

Hugging a photo album to his side with his stump, Ames, who'd watched CJ's every move since he'd entered the store, surprised CJ by calling out, "Help you with somethin', son?"

"No. Just looking," CJ said, trying to sound casual.

The seasoned World War II veteran, who now stood just a few feet away from CJ, nodded and took a long, hard look at his customer. A look of recognition crossed Wiley's face as he took in the strangely vacant look in the young black man's eyes.

"Well, look all you want and let me know if you need some help. Been in before?" he asked as an afterthought, his eyes never moving off CJ.

"A couple of times," CJ said quickly, fearful that anything but the truth might expose his motives.

"Well, go on with your lookin'. I'm around if you need me." Wiley turned and headed toward a counter near the front of the store. Halfway to his destination, he glanced back over his shoulder and thought to himself, *No mistakin', that boy's got invisible damage.*

CJ continued staring at the wall of art, taking in the black-and-white photographs, watercolors, and pastels, most of them depicting classic Western scenes. There were scenes of rodeo cowboys, a photograph of two cowboys on horseback chasing a steer, a painting of an angler shaded by a canopy of cottonwoods fishing in a remote mountain stream, and finally a photo of a startled hunter, shotgun at the ready, watching half a dozen sage grouse flush. Once again the word *home* flashed through CJ's subconscious. Remembering his purpose, he walked over to the spot where the electrical box and loose tiles should have been. As he reached out to adjust one of the photographs, as if to make certain that he wasn't looking at a mirage, Ames reappeared, ghostlike and silent.

"So, whattaya think?" Ames asked, beaming.

"Nice."

"I like to think so. I call it my Wall of the West. The boss let me do it. Said it gave the place a sense of character. Damn thing even faces west." He watched as CJ's eyes darted from photograph to photograph. "They're not for sale if you're lookin' to buy. All of 'em are by local artists, most of 'em down on their luck. Mostly they're here for the enjoyin'. Sorta like life."

"They're great. How'd you get the idea?" CJ asked, thinking about the missing license plate and electrical box.

Wiley chuckled. "DURA, them urban redevelopment folks, gave the idea to me a year or so back when they blew the Cooper Building over on Seventeenth Street to smithereens. The explosion nearly took down that wall you're eyein'. Had to just about rebuild the sucker. Bricks, mortar, a hell of a lot of tuck-pointin', and, of course, new drywall and electrical."

"I see," said CJ, imagining the hidden license plate flying out from behind the tiles and crashing to the floor, its delicate porcelain fracturing. "Find anything behind the wall?"

"Not really." Ames cocked an eye and looked CJ up and down. "Least, not anything of importance. Sure you don't need my help with anything?" he asked with a hint of suspicion in his tone.

"Nope."

"Well, then, admire the wall as long as you like. After awhile it sorta grows on you. I'm around if you need me." Wiley sauntered toward the store's front cash register. Halfway to his destination, he glanced back at CJ, eyed the spot on the sleeve of CJ's pea-coat where the first-class gunner's-mate stripes had once been and thought, *Boy's got damage for sure.*

Realizing that the license plate was lost to him forever, CJ locked his gaze on a photograph of two cowboys branding a calf.

One cowboy had the calf's head pinned to the dirt with a knee while the other, smoke rising from his branding iron, seared the calf's right hindquarter. Thinking that all some people might see was brutality, unless of course they'd been to war, he turned to leave. As he pivoted, he caught a glimpse of a grainy black-and-white photograph near the bottom of the wall. Bending to take a closer look, he recognized that the strangely out-of-place photo was filled with the image of a World War II–vintage Sherman tank. Three American soldiers stood beside the tank's turret, one smoking a cigarette, one staring aimlessly into space, and one drinking coffee. Even after more than two decades, there could be no mistaking the identity of the man staring into space. It was a slightly thinner, gaunt-looking Wiley Ames.

CJ stared at the photo for several more seconds before walking toward the front of the store. When he reached the front checkout counter, where Ames stood organizing a handful of receipts, he asked, "That you in that tank photo on the wall?"

"Yep," Ames said, in response to a question he'd been asked hundreds of times.

"Thought so."

"Long time ago," said Ames.

"Bet it never goes away."

"Not really. But you move on."

"Guess so," a suddenly glassy-eyed CJ said, offering Ames a two-fingered salute and heading toward the door. "See you around."

CJ was six blocks away when Ames left his post behind the cash register and headed toward a glassed-in display case near the center of the store. He wasn't quite certain why he'd made a beeline for that particular case, except that CJ's words, "Find anything behind the wall?" continued to resonate in his head. As he stooped to open

one of the case's misaligned rear doors, intent on retrieving the
1914 porcelain license plate that had been coughed up from behind
his Wall of the West the day DURA had blown up the Cooper
Building a year and a half earlier, he found himself shaking his
head. Eyeing the flawless antique license plate, he had the strange
sense that he and the young black man who'd just left were somehow connected. He couldn't put his finger on exactly why or how or
for what reason, but he knew it had something to do with his wall
of art and the look he'd seen in the young man's eyes when he'd first
walked into the store. A lost, hollow look yearning for explanation.
A look that was identical to the look in his own eyes all those years
ago when he'd stood next to a tank turret oblivious to the falling
snow in a German forest just hours before losing his left arm in the
Battle of the Bulge. A look that told him that he and the young
black man had something very much in common.

BEGINNINGS: 1982
DIANE MOTT DAVIDSON

1980s

Beginnings: 1982

DIANE MOTT DAVIDSON

ARCH STUMBLED ONTO THE BODY OF MANNY TRENT AT DUSK the night before Thanksgiving. A heavy confetti of snow was falling all over Denver. An hour earlier, we'd left our house in Aspen Meadow, forty miles to the west, in what felt like an onrushing storm. Panicked, fearful for reasons other than weather, I'd hustled Arch into our Jeep and just taken off. No boots. No hats. No plans.

"I'm sorry, hon." I lifted him onto the curb of Larimer Street. "I forgot your—"

"Don't worry about it, Mom." Arch brushed a thick layer of snow off the front of the too-large Broncos jacket I'd found at our local secondhand store. "I slipped."

At five years of age, our son was already in the habit of assuring me that things were not my fault. It was not my fault that my husband, Dr. John Richard Korman, did not give me enough money to buy us adequate winter clothes; not my fault that John Richard thought my housekeeping was inadequate; not my fault that the farm I usually bought our discounted Thanksgiving turkey from had closed early. With some trepidation, I'd informed John Richard that we would not have our usual fresh bird for the holiday; unfortunately, everything left at the grocery store would be budget-breaking twenty-pound monsters.

I'd heard the click of John Richard's toolbox opening. I knew what that meant, of course. I'd hollered I was going out to look for a half-price turkey, grabbed Arch, and raced away.

As Arch and I had stumbled along, my right thumb—freezing inside old garden gloves—ached with cold. What had driven us from home—that click of the toolbox opening—was the fact that John Richard did not use a wrench or screwdriver to fix things. The last time he'd used his hammer, he'd broken my now-throbbing thumb in three places. So when I delivered the news about the turkey farm and heard the toolbox snap open, I knew it was time to get out of Dodge.

"Mom," said Arch, his elfin face turned to me in adultlike alarm, "are you okay?"

"I'm fine." My shoulders slumped heavily. Around us, the snow fell.

Just last night, John Richard had insisted it had been two weeks since I'd changed the sheets. I'd told him he was wrong and been rewarded with a punch to the eye. This morning, before the turkey-farm fiasco, I'd dabbed concealer on the blackening skin, to little avail.

"I landed on somebody," Arch said now, the hood of his jacket askew on his straw-colored hair. His hands in their mismatched mittens pointed at a lump at the edge of the street.

I peered down. "It's a snowdrift."

"No, Mom. Somebody tripped on the curb." The two of us stared at the immobile, snow-ensconced body. "Maybe Yolanda can help us," Arch said.

Yolanda was a friend. She also worked doing food prep at Laffite's, an upscale French restaurant at the corner of Fourteenth and Larimer. She had offered me a job "whenever you decide to leave that s.o.b." Of course, since John Richard had told me repeatedly that I was *good for nothing* and that *no one will ever hire you*, it had occurred to me, as I'd driven blindly to Denver, that I could finally take Yolanda up on her offer. I just didn't know what I'd be doing, where Arch and I would stay, or how I would keep us going. I also had no idea how chefs, with their notoriously big egos, would deal with a twenty-five-year-old housewife who had no professional food experience and, to make things worse, had brought her five-year-old son along for the ride.

"It's a man." Arch reached down to the unmoving slab. "Uh-oh." He held up one of his mittens. I blinked snow from my eyes. Light from street lamps illuminated the mitten, which was covered with blood.

We hustled along to Laffite's, where a partylike atmosphere throbbed in the crowded dining room, in spite of—or perhaps because of—the storm. I looked in awe at the red-flocked wallpaper, the red-leather booths, the glittering people all seeming to be having a wonderful time. The last time I'd had a wonderful time, I'd been making sushi for Arch's kindergarten class.

"Do you have a reservation?" the maître d' demanded.

"I need an ambulance," I squawked. "Someone's hurt outside."

"Hurt?" The maître d's face was pasty-white. He pinched his thin mustache. "Or passed out, drunk?"

"Is Yolanda here?" I asked impatiently.

The maître d' lifted his pointed chin. "Is this drunk a relative of hers?" When I returned his stare, he shrugged. "You can go around back."

"That guy was mean," Arch whispered. We made our way out of the opulent scarlet room. A few swankily dressed patrons gave us curious glances. *What do that woman in the drab trench coat and her kid in the orange jacket want in here? I want you to stop staring at me*, I felt like screaming. But of course I had no voice for that, had little voice for anything these days.

"Yolanda," I said with relief, when Arch and I had traipsed up the unplowed alley, now almost a foot deep in snow.

"Arch! Goldy!" Yolanda was a beautiful young woman, the daughter of Cuban immigrants. She had a heart-wrenching smile and a tumble of dark hair that escaped every attempt at a ponytail. We'd met at an ecumenical church picnic, and I'd invited her to teach my Sunday school class to make Cuban bread. Arch adored Yolanda.

"Wait," I began, before Arch and Yolanda could visit, "there's a problem."

Yolanda brought us into the warm, bustling kitchen, where I told her about the body. She frowned. "The radio just announced that police and hospitals aren't responding to anything but emergencies."

"This qualifies." I got on the phone to an operator.

"It smells great in here," Arch said to Yolanda, who asked if he was hungry. Of course, he was.

"Do you want a steak?" Yolanda asked.

"Do you make your own béarnaise?" Arch asked, all seriousness. My son, the epicure.

"Do we ever," said Yolanda.

Eventually the police showed up—driving snowmobiles, no less—and had me lead them to the man still lying in the street. I answered their questions—when had we found him, did we know him, where would we be if they had more questions—and then I trudged back through the ever-deepening snow to Laffite's. The police assured me they'd get medical help for the man.

In the kitchen, Yolanda darkly informed me that this was the second time in a month the police had shown up at the restaurant. The first time, they'd said they were investigating illegal sales of prescription painkillers in lower downtown. Anyone with information was supposed to call them, but as far as Yolanda knew, no one had.

I checked on Arch. He had been adopted by the executive chef himself, André Hibbard, a fortyish, prematurely gray-haired emigré who still had a heavy French accent. My throat clenched as I listened to my son's questions. Would the restaurant be serving Thanksgiving dinner tomorrow? Did they have an extra fresh turkey that we could take home? The farm we usually went to had closed early. This brought a puzzled look from André and laughter from Yolanda.

André assigned me to trim and poach asparagus. Not far away, Arch watched as André used a blowtorch to caramelize the top of a crème brûlée. Then my son frowned as he expertly cracked the topping with a spoon. The servers marveled at Arch's big appetite, then said, Yes, he could help them clear the tables.

I trimmed and poached, trimmed and poached. I felt remarkably at home. The only dark cloud appeared when the sous-chef, a tall, heavy, very imposing fellow named David Bertuzzi, tripped over Arch as my son was bringing a bag of sugared pecans to André, as requested.

Bertuzzi howled, picked himself up off the floor, and yelled, "What the hell is this kid doing in my kitchen?"

"This is *my* kitchen," André replied swiftly, his voice sharp. A shiver raced down my spine. Before I could move, André helped Arch off the floor and took the bag of nuts. Bertuzzi said he was going for a cigarette break and marched off to the exit.

"David's a screamer," Yolanda said as soon as he disappeared. "He's just been here a few weeks. Everyone else is nice, except for the maître d', Thomas. He's a pretentious jerk who we're pretty sure helps himself to the servers' tips."

"Doesn't anybody stop him?"

"We can't catch him." Yolanda glanced at her watch. "We'll close soon. Then you and Arch come stay with me. Can you wash pots now?"

I could. It hardly felt as if time was passing, except that my back began to ache. Suddenly, the police swung through the doors into the kitchen.

It seemed the man in the street was dead. His name was Manny Trent, and he'd been a sometime-dishwasher at Laffite's. The police said they had questions for us.

The cops pulled the workers off, one by one, to the closed oyster bar to ask when the last time was that anyone had seen or talked to Trent. Yolanda was crying. She told me Manny had an old Chevy, and when he hadn't shown up tonight, she'd just assumed his engine wouldn't turn over, or that his tires were too bald to make it through the snow.

"He was saving up for a new car," she said. "He had a second job, but he wouldn't tell me which restaurant had hired him."

"Mom!" said Arch excitedly, running in from the dining room. He held up a fistful of cash. "Look at all this money I found on the tables! Now we can afford a big turkey!"

"This brat!" Thomas fumed, striding fast on Arch's heels. "He's stealing the servers' tips!"

I snatched Arch to protect him from Thomas while Yolanda smoothly retrieved the money from Arch's clenched hand.

"He's a kid," Yolanda said. "He doesn't know about tips."

"He *should*." Thomas's voice was stubborn.

"You gonna teach him?" Yolanda demanded.

"Mister Sardukian," the detectives summoned Thomas, who left to be questioned.

"Don't worry about the tips," Yolanda reassured me. "The waiters and waitresses are supposed to pool them. With Thomas talking to the cops, Arch probably saved our people money tonight!"

"Mom, I'm sorry." Arch buried his face in my shoulder. "Will this get you in trouble?"

"No, hon."

There was a pause while he snuffled. "I saw something," he said in a tiny voice, his cheek next to my neck. "But I don't want that to get you in trouble, either."

"It won't." Like Arch, I kept my voice very low. "What was it?"

"When André sent me to the pantry to get flour? It was hot in the kitchen, so I barely opened the back door. I saw that mean guy in the alley. He had André's blowtorch."

"Which mean guy?"

"The cook who yelled at me. He wasn't smoking a cigarette, and he wasn't cooking anything. He was trying to burn something."

My body chilled. As unobtrusively as possible, I sidled up to a policewoman and asked if she would accompany me and my son to the bathroom. She nodded.

In the ladies' room, I tried first not to look at my black eye. Then I avoided gawking at the golden swan faucets.

The policewoman said to me, "We haven't talked to *you* yet."

"No."

"You want to tell me how you got that black eye?"

"Not really. Actually, it's my son who has something to tell you."

Arch repeated his tale. The policewoman then radioed one of the detectives in the kitchen, who barreled into the ladies' room, looking as uncomfortable as I felt. Arch told his story once more.

The detective said this would help, that they'd search outside for the blowtorch, a weapon, and whatever Bertuzzi had been burning. They'd question the sous-chef again, see if anyone else had witnessed him burning something.

The policewoman brought us back to the kitchen and said she'd stay with us. Two detectives kept Bertuzzi occupied while a third disappeared. An hour later, the last detective returned and said he'd found the blowtorch, a bloody switchblade, and the remains of a scorched notebook, and—a very lucky break—a woman from a nearby apartment building had seen Bertuzzi, whom she recognized from Laffite's, trying to burn something in back of the restaurant. What with all the snow falling, he'd seemed to be having a hard time.

Two detectives led Bertuzzi away in handcuffs.

Manny Trent, the remaining detective told us, had been a police informant. Trent had been keeping a notebook on people selling prescription painkillers. When the cops had taken Trent's body tonight, the notebook, which Manny had kept on him at all times, had been missing.

Yolanda said they were closing. Did I still want to come stay with her? she asked. Her apartment was within walking distance. I hesitated.

"Can I take you somewhere?" the policewoman asked me. "It's really snowing hard out there."

Arch tugged on my apron. His large brown eyes implored me. He said, "I miss Dad."

I sighed. "Can you take us to our house in Aspen Meadow?" I asked the policewoman. "I'm sorry—"

"Don't be. Your son just helped us clear a murder and drug case. I'll be out front."

Yolanda shook her head. I hugged her and said I was sorry.

André beckoned to me; Yolanda held onto Arch. The chef smiled and said, "The owner fired the maître d'. I told him we caught Thomas being very mean to your son." Then André pressed a wad of cash into my hand. "That's for tonight." I started to protest, but he stopped me. "Arch tells me you teach Sunday school." When I nodded, he went on, "Your son witnessed a very bad man trying to destroy evidence."

"Yes," I said. "But the police won't call Arch to testify unless they absolutely have to. They promised."

André shook his head impatiently. "I'm not talking about Bertuzzi, or about court. I'm talking about that word. *Witness*."

"Yes," I said tentatively. Sunday school. Not going to court. What was this gentle chef getting at?

"Do you know the Greek word for *witness*?" André asked me.

"Yes," I replied. "*Martyr*."

"Exactly." André nodded. His calloused fingers brushed my swollen eye. Not used to a tender touch, I winced.

"I'm fine."

"You're not," André replied matter-of-factly. "You think your son is not noticing what is happening in your home. But your son notices everything." I swallowed. "Listen to me, Goldy," André said. "In the next year or two, I am leaving Laffite's. I will open my own restaurant. You have a job with me. I will be catering, too—"

"I don't know anything about—"

André held up his hand. "I will teach you. You can work for me, make enough money for you and Arch."

I was skeptical. "Enough—"

"Yes," André interrupted. "Catering is not easier than restaurant work, only different. You make your own schedule. Goldy," André said, his voice soothing, "you do not have to be a *martyr*." He gave it the Greek pronunciation.

"I will come," I said suddenly. "When you open the new restaurant."

André nodded, then lifted his hand in farewell, as did Yolanda. And I, well, I turned back to Arch, and back, alas, to home. But as the policewoman's snowmobile churned westward through the blizzard, I clutched Arch, and something else. I had, finally—on what was now technically Thanksgiving—a sliver of something in my heart, a small slice of a feeling to which I was unaccustomed.

Hope.

THE COLOR OF THE IMPRESSION

LAURA PRITCHETT

2000s

The Color
of the Impression

LAURA PRITCHETT

I WAS ICE-SKATING ON THE POND, THE PUPPY BOUNDING AROUND next to me, leaping at my legs in adoration and joy, and it was this exuberance that caused us to collide. I ran over the pup's paw with the blade of my skate, and her yelp pierced the air as I plunged forward, right into the boat that I leave, upside down, next to the pond. My head hit the chine of the boat, the boat being a little plywood number I made myself. So many things happen in such a moment: I thought, *Oh, this hurts*, and tipped my head back so the blood in my nose would run backward, and my eyes sought out the puppy, who was limping over to me, leaving bloody footprints on the ice, including one red swipe where she slipped stepping over the push broom I'd used to clear away the snow.

I knew I was fine but that the puppy should get to the vet, for her prints were pure blood now, as if her foot were a brush sopped with red paint. I stood and skated over to the edge of the pond, which was where I'd left my hiking boots, and it took me some time to unlace the skates since my fingers were thick with cold and the laces themselves were hard, but finally I could gather the pup in my arms and carry her to my truck. I was dizzy but told myself, as I do during difficult times, *Ah, shut up and wait it out*, because the pain would pass and I believed then that fleeting moments shouldn't get much attention, though now I understand that they are in fact what make up my life.

There was an old towel under the pickup's seat, and the last time I'd used it was to rub a newborn calf into life—he'd been plopped down, wet and slick, into the snow, and his mama was doing a half-assed job of licking him warm. But the calf lived. As I started the truck, I put one hand on the pup's side to hold her down into the seat and apologized, as I did with the calf, for the ways life can surprise you with pain.

That was the last moment I remember of my old self, my self that had not yet met Ruben. The next moment I was in a train wreck, which is to say, I was in the wrong place at the wrong time. I could not have avoided it, even if I'd tried, which I did not.

Ruben was not the vet. Ruben was the vet's nephew, and judging from his looks you'd guess he was about twenty-five. A child. In comparison. But Ruben looked at me as I told my story, looked at me for longer than one would expect. His eyes were very dark, he was Mexican, with eyes that were like liquid.

The puppy was on the examining table, and Ruben tilted his head to consider the paw, and he said, "Name?"

"Well. I don't know, I just got her. I call her Pup."

Ruben's eyes moved from the pup's foot to my head. "Your forehead. You could use a coupla stitches." But he said it without conviction, because we both knew I wouldn't be driving off the mountain and into town for three small stitches.

"Do you have any of that glue that sticks your skin together?" I asked. "The cut doesn't hurt. No, that's a lie, actually it does. We humans do that all the time! Lie about pain, I mean. Do you know that glue I'm talking about?"

It might be too much to believe that's all it took. Although maybe not: perhaps it's uncommon to run into a person who's more or less a stranger but you know has interests that align with yours—animals, outdoors, tenderness in a world that is without—and then to have your breath taken away for no other reason than his searching eyes, his smile, and some sort of quiet sadness buzzing about him. Perhaps, on top of this, you know you are a bit off-kilter, and that the outside world has a tendency to scowl at you since you cannot quite maneuver through life as they do, and perhaps you know that there are only a handful of people who are going to think that's fine and maybe even preferable. Perhaps all this can happen, and it is not love, at that particular instant, but it is the beginning of it, or at least contains the potential.

Ruben said, "Yes, glue, in a minute," like that was the conclusion he'd already come to. "Your pup has a deep laceration, but the

tendon isn't severed. It's a full-skin-thickness cut, though, so Victor will use skin staples, wrap it, antibiotic. Clean cut, though. Nice cut for a cut." He shrugged. "I know who you are. You're the woman who helps out at the Vreeland Ranch. You live up the canyon. You're their ranch hand, right?"

"Yes."

"You have a lot of animals." This he said with a certain amount of admiration.

"Yes, lots of animals."

"You have bees, you sell honey."

"Yes, I do," I said. "People think I'm crazy. But I'm not very crazy! My neighbor, Wendell, calls my place a Damn Petting Zoo. I told him he had so much junk on his property that I could get tetanus just by looking."

Ruben chuckled and said, "The truth is, Victor is at home. Archangels are visiting him today." He looked at me to see if I understood, which I did. Victor is schizophrenic and delusional, and on some days functional and some days not, and during some years he's fared well, and during others he's disappeared completely. Last year, for instance, someone from the mountain found him on Larimer Street, in Denver, sleeping next to a dumpster, and they brought him home, and since then we have all been more careful to protect this Victor, this vet who talks to God, who sees patterns and light in ways that we do not. So I knew I had the option of driving forty miles down the mountain or letting Ruben take over, this vet tech, this nephew, this quiet, beautiful man.

"Well, can you do it?" I ventured. "Because I don't like town much."

I put my hand over my mouth. You might think I have problems with silence, but in fact I do not. In fact I spend most of my time in silence and the silence of my body is basically in equilibrium with the silence of the world. It's only when I get with other people that I become nervous, I don't know why, except to say that it's a little hard to clarify some things about yourself to yourself, even when you have long conversations with yourself about yourself in the silence.

When Ruben was done, and the pup was standing on the floor, wagging her tail, holding up her bandaged paw, Ruben washed his hands and stood in front of me. He squinted at my forehead. Cleaned the wound with a cotton ball dipped in something. Dabbed on a bit of glue from his finger to my forehead. I tried (successfully, I might add!) to breathe quietly and not let the tears slip, for suddenly I was feeling very alone, that buzzing heavy terror of a space when you recognize that you are alone and that you are going to die alone. This was bad timing for such a moment to descend, but I managed under the weight of it all.

Ruben said, "You cut your lip," to which I nodded. For a moment I thought that perhaps we both wanted him to kiss it, to apply another kind of healing. But such a thing is not allowed, of course, by the invisible forces that operate this world. These invisible forces have too much power, if you ask me. If only the world could be less influenced by them, then their potency would naturally decrease.

Ruben put on a Band-Aid and his fingers stayed an extra moment as he pushed down the plastic tabs. He said, *"Mucho gusto,* it's nice to meet you, Lillie."

That was the moment that became slowed down in my mind. Because he knew my name, though I had not said it. And because I am not a person who is ever touched by another human, and so I could not help but like it a great deal.

"El gusto es mio, Ruben," I whispered.

His eyes lit up in surprise at my bit of offered Spanish. Then he nodded and directed me, with a wave of his arm, to the front of the clinic, where I paid my bill. Then I left.

That is the bulk of my story. By the time I got to my truck, with the puppy in my arms, I was wondering what the best course of action is when one is in a train wreck. Run away from the wreckage? Or stay in the danger and heat?

I managed to stay away from town for quite some time, and then Victor shot himself. Finally the archangels had been too much. They had been in cahoots with God, setting up various mental obstacle courses to see if Victor was worthy and in the end, Victor felt he wasn't, and he took Ruben's Colt .45 from Ruben's truck and put it in his mouth.

Ruben felt bad about it being his gun, but I called Ruben and told him, along with many other people, Victor would have found a way no matter what. I also told Ruben that I did not feel anything but agreement about this suicide because had I been in Victor's position I no doubt would've walked out in a field, just like he did, and shot myself, too, and indeed, in my most off-kilter moments I've thought about doing just that.

It was getting to be spring, now, and the roads were slushy around the cemetery, and our footprints went down to the earth and left watery brown marks. To get to the funeral, I caught a ride down the canyon with Wendell, and on the way Wendell and I conversed in such a way as to confirm for each other that we did not like each other; he thought I was a scattered and strange woman, and I thought him a dull and stupid man.

"I'm in love with a man," I told him. "It's going to take a lot of effort and erosion to get rid of this feeling." I said this so I could get it out of my system. How many of us are going around telling the truth to the wrong person? Wendell took it as one more piece of evidence of my malformed character, and I took my confession as a needed relief to have voiced my love to someone, somewhere, at some point in time.

The person I hoped to see at the service, of course, was Ruben. I'm honest enough to admit that even at a funeral of someone who had doctored my goats and peacock and cats, I was selfishly thinking of love. Ruben was dressed in black jeans and roper boots and seeing him this way made my heart feel as if it were suffocating; I had to avert my eyes, actually, so as to find some relief. What I did not realize then, but came to understand during the course of the after-funeral gathering, as I kept my hand over my mouth and listened to people talk, was that I was possibly saying goodbye to Ruben as well. Because it is illegal for someone who does not have a degree and license to practice vet medicine, and now that Victor was gone, there was no way that Ruben could keep the clinic open. I did hear it mentioned, however, that Ruben, who, wisely enough, refused to go to school to prove what he already knew (and thus refused to give in to those invisible forces that operate this world), might just doctor animals as a "friend who was helping out" and a person might pay Ruben for his help. As I listened to a dozen conversations, I knew where Ruben was at all moments, which caused me to wonder if love is simply keeping track of a person.

When Ruben came up to me and asked about my puppy, as I knew he would, it was not as I had hoped. There was nothing in his eyes that showed I was alive to him in some unique way. Perhaps he saw my reaction to this because he tried to say something nice. He said, "I never asked you about ice-skating. But I imagined you, skating alone, on the Vreelands' pond on that foggy day, yes?" and when I nodded he continued, "It's rather pretty, the picture I have in my mind. Until the puppy got hurt, that is."

I almost said the following: "This love is invisible but it is very, very heavy."

What I said instead was, "My horse has an odd swelling in its chest and maybe ought to be looked at?"

"It's probably Pigeon disease," he said. "A new thing with horses. They get it from bacteria in the dirt."

"When I push my hand into my horse's chest, where the swelling is, there is the impression of my hand for a moment. Ruben, am I imagining this?"

He looked at me truly, then, and gave his answer: No, you are not imagining this, but no, there is no way for this disease (called love) to be resolved in this particular case. Right then I knew how exhausting it would be, waiting for a peace that was never going to come. And I took notice of my ache, and realized it had a strange, buzzing hum that could nearly burst my eardrums apart.

Pretend, if you will, that this is a story, and that it ends like this: There is a woman, some figure in the far distance, a shape that's hard to make out, and she has a task ahead of her, which is to expel a feeling as best she can, or at the very least maneuver it so that the place it occupies inside her is comfortable, or if not comfortable, then bearable. I laughed, for what an odd thing to do to love!

I went home and began to walk alongside the edge of the pond, my puppy darting in front of me, and I noticed that in certain places, the spring snow had formed ridges of intricate crystals that jutted up at an angle. I was surprised to discover, if I squinted my eyes, the degree to which patterns create snow. Then I considered the degree to which colors create snow. Then I considered the degree to which light creates snow. After I came to, I continued walking, and continued to create the collateral damage we all do as we go through life, but then I could no longer crush those snow crystals with my feet in such a clumsy manner, and so I retraced my steps carefully. I walked back to the pond and stared into the melting ice sheaf. While I stared, I kept hearing noises at the water's edge, and I thought an animal was perhaps moving about in the dry grasses. It took me some time to realize the noise came from the ice melting at the edges, slipping into the water below. So I sat in the grass at the edge and watched the crystals slip into the absorbing water, and sometimes I helped it along by gently brushing and dabbing the slush down with a stick that had been left to rest, kindly enough, beside me.

Future

HEIRLOOMS

Robert Pogue Ziegler

Heirlooms

ROBERT POGUE ZIEGLER

Peanut sat on the cracked concrete stoop like Alice on the mushroom, bare feet folded under her rump, faded SpongeBob T-shirt hooked over her knees. She scooped handfuls of loose charcoal from a brazier made from the bottom third of a rusted fifty-gal drum and pressed it into a heap of wet cotton set on a scrap of tin siding laid before her. Her sunburned nose wrinkled with determination as she beat at the mixture with tiny palms. Teresa watched her and marveled how the girl resembled her own mother.

"Like that, Mama?" Peanut asked, glancing up suddenly, fer-retlike, to catch Teresa's eyes on her.

Teresa smiled. "*Si*, baby, but more charcoal. It's the charcoal that cleans the water. Pack in as much as the cotton will hold."

The mid-July sun hammered down, lighting the corn tassels like molten gold. Cicadas rattled in the heat.

"Look, Mama. *Perros de la basura*." Peanut pointed to where two children, naked and sun browned, skulked at the intersection where the cul de sac joined a meandering suburban through street. A boy and girl, probably brother and sister, not much older than Peanut, part of the pack of orphans who had dogged the caravan from as far south as Baton Rouge and hovered now like flies around the caravan's summer squat, thieving gardens and trash heaps. They prowled the cul de sac's entrance, eyeing the irregular rows of immature corn laid between the crumbling sidewalk and the circle of abandoned three-bedroom houses that were at the tag end of decades-long collapse. Their bare feet made quick, tender steps on the searing pavement.

"*No les hagas caso*, Pea," Teresa said. "Just so long as they stay away from our corn."

She bent and sank her spade into the dry dirt between rows of corn she and Peanut had planted together earlier in the summer. Her calloused fingers sifted a clump of earth, found a moist worm, plucked it, and dropped it into a rusty soup can nearly full with worms. She repeated the process, up and down the rows: spade and sift, harvest worms, pull weeds when she found them.

Occasionally, she coughed.

She had learned to surrender when it came—it hurt less that way. She pulled long black hair back from her face like someone preparing to vomit and let the spasms wrack her with a sound like tearing silk. When the coughing subsided, her lungs felt as hot and coarse as asphalt. She stood and stretched, pressing palms into the small of her back.

"*No esta bien*, Mama," Peanut scolded. "*Esta peorando*. You wait till we're on the road. You can't be sick when we got real vegetables coming on."

Real vegetables. Not the ubiquitous, flavorless gen-built corn, but real heirlooms. Tomatoes, habaneros, green peppers, cilantro, basil, cucumbers, delicata and acorn squash—all hidden, growing behind the dilapidated three-bed, camouflaged by the remains of a privacy fence covered in bindweed.

"*¡Callate!* Lupia. Keep your voice down." Teresa's tone was harsh. For years she had collected the seeds, waiting for a cool summer after a long spring to plant, and this summer, finally, her garden grew. It was the only wealth she had ever known, and she intended to keep it secret. "Finish that filter if you don't want to go to bed thirsty."

She felt a sudden hot pressure behind her eyes, a fever that had touched intermittently for days. It enveloped her head, haloing everything in fiery gauze. A chill moved up her spine. She closed her eyes, waiting for it to pass, but it stayed and after a few minutes she resigned herself to it. Turning once more to the corn, she shivered and sweat and dug.

Her mind seemed to dream while she worked. She thought of her mother, lying in a cot set out on the hardpan plain, burning with malaria beneath the yellow Oklahoma sky, watching dry summer days turn into night and back again. "I can feel the

world turning, Teresa," she'd said, sweat beading her face. She had clutched a Virgin Mother idol, fashioned from a corncob and precisely cut pieces of soda can, close to her chest and prayed: "I accept from your hands whatever it may please you to send me this night..." Teresa had kept the idol after her mother died, and now it stood on the mantel over the useless fireplace in the three-bed's living room, where she and Peanut slept. Every night Teresa placed a lit candle at the idol's feet, thought of her mother, and, in the warmth of the candle's glow, sang *Una rata vieja* until Peanut slept.

"Leave our corn alone, *¡perros mugrientos!*" Teresa stood to find Peanut on her feet, T-shirt hanging to her ankles, shaking both fists at the two orphans. They had sneaked up the street and were now picking immature ears from the edge of Teresa's corn patch.

Teresa advanced on them, spade held rapierlike before her. "*¡Tocan mi elote y voy a cortarles en fertilizante!*"

The boy, maybe eleven years old, all ribs, sunburn, and grime, stared back defiantly. The girl hid behind him, peering cautiously around his bony hip with huge, septic eyes. She was barely older than Peanut, seven or eight, and her belly was swollen. Hunger, and probably dysentery. Teresa leveled the spade at the boy's nose.

"Don't think I won't."

"Don't think you will," said the boy. They stood motionless. Dry wind kicked up dust around them.

"Mama?"

"Stay on the porch, Lupia." Teresa leaned in close to the boy. "I'll give you a limp you'll keep forever." She made it sound like a promise. The boy looked uncertain, but did not move. Teresa raised the spade high and for an instant held it, poised to slash down. Then she coughed. She tried to hold it back, a small dry hack. But all at once her lungs heaved and she doubled over, seized by a ragged series of expirations, the worst she had ever had. She wondered if it was possible for her lungs to turn inside out and balloon from her mouth.

The boy backed away. "You bad sick, lady." He grabbed his sister by the hand, turned, and together they loped like hungry coyotes down the potholed asphalt.

When the coughing passed, Teresa found herself on her knees in the dirt. She stood, staggered, steadied herself. She found Peanut watching her, face taught with mute fear. Teresa turned her head, spat, and watched as a bright red globule of blood the size of her thumbnail quivered for a moment before sinking into the dry earth.

"I need you to take me into the city on your wagon." Teresa stood in the garage's cavernous opening, watching Hondo Loco work a soldering iron against a coil of copper pipes attached to a patched, three-hundred-gal plastic tank. A corn still, whether for diesel or alcohol she was not sure.

"What makes you think I can get into the city?" Hondo asked without looking at her. A makeshift windmill whined overhead, mounted beside the garage on a long wooden mast. Old extension cords ran from it to a crate of salvaged twelve-volts, which powered a jerry-rigged stack of amps, naked hard drive, and speaker cone, from which thumped midcentury Chinese dub.

"*¿Piensas que soy tonta?* Everybody knows you go in. Wasn't no prairie saint who gave you those scars."

Hondo stopped soldering. He wore a faded blue tank top, and tats ran the course of his long, sinewed arms, interrupted by several stamp-size squares of newly grafted pink skin—some doctors paid a good price for gene-mining. He pursed his lips and pushed a thick gray dreadlock out of his face. "Twenty-five percent."

Teresa stifled a cough. "How 'bout just doing me the favor?"

"Ain't no favors on our side of the glass, baby girl. You and little Lupia can get by on two-thirds of what you harvest. Twenty-five percent for you is surplus, easy."

"I ain't your baby girl. Ten, and I'll help you make diesel after the harvest."

Hondo thought for a moment, then shook his head slowly. "I hear you coughing in the night from three houses down, *chica*. You need a doctor." His eyes, Teresa saw, were not without sympathy. But he did not bend.

"Okay," she said finally. "A quarter. When can we go?"

Hondo grinned, showing gaps where front teeth had once been. "How's right now?"

His wagon was the wooden flatbed of a twen-cen cargo truck chopped free from its cab and driven by an electric motor connected to the front wheels by a motorcycle chain. Teresa sat at the front, cradling Peanut against her chest while Hondo stood at the back, manhandling the wagon with a tiller welded to the rear axle. They rumbled north and west, winding through neighborhoods of empty brick ranch houses overrun by prairie grass. Twice they stopped and Hondo fired a homemade slingshot at prairie dogs or rabbits, and twice, cursing, he missed. They reached old Highway 6 and Hondo, straining hard at the tiller, turned them slowly left, straight west.

Denver rose before them, a monolithic cube of glass that shone like a block of amber in the vicious midday sun. To the south rose the chipped gold dome of the old Capitol building, gleaming like a gold-capped tooth, and behind it all stood the Rockies, dark as a wall of thunderheads.

They encountered more people as they drew nearer the city. Shanty and tent towns filled the parking lots of burned-out strip malls. The reek of raw sewage assailed them, and throngs of people, many of them children and many of them naked, idled by the roadside watching with gaunt, expressionless faces as the wagon rumbled past.

"Who are they, Mama?" asked Peanut, her eyes wide with wonder.

"They're refugees, Pea."

"What are refugees?"

"*Carroneros*. People who can't feed themselves."

"Like that boy and girl who tried to steal our corn?"

"*Si*, but these people want the city's garbage, not ours."

Peanut grew pensive. "So we're not *carroneros*, are we, Mama?"

"No, baby." Teresa pulled Peanut close and thought of their secret bounty burgeoning now behind the house. And then she coughed.

Isoniazid. Rifampin. Pyrazinamide. Ethambutol. The doctor on Larimer Street had meted out the envelopes full of pills into Teresa's hand. It reminded her of communion. The pills made her sick to her stomach, but she took them anyway, twice each day for two months.

The cough persisted.

Thunderheads built in the afternoons, Lupia would point at them over the hissing canning pot. "Monsoons are coming, Mama. We won't be able to finish the canning." But they did.

The tomatoes came on first, undersized but succulent. Teresa showed Peanut the way her mother had taught her how to eat a tomato. A lick, a pinch of salt, heaven. They built a canning pot together out of a fifty-gal drum that they set over a fire pit in the backyard. Teresa tended the fire most of every day through late August and early September, slumped with fever against the back wall of the house, poking at the flames with a stick while Lupia stripped wood from the unoccupied house next door. Every hour or so she coughed and spit a bright string of blood into the dirt at her feet.

When the tomatoes were finished, the cucumbers came on, then the squash, thick as one of Lupia's legs. They gathered the seeds from the biggest and healthiest vegetables and set them in rows on the cracked, south-facing window sills. After the seeds dried, Teresa folded them into paper, which she labeled with a tiny nub of pencil before packing them in jars. These they buried in the basement.

The monsoons arrived as a steady, tranquil rain in mid-September, the day Teresa took the last of the pills. Two days later, it was as though a dam burst inside her body. The cough filled her lungs and the fever pulled her down like a hot, wet net. She lay on her bed mat beside the cold fireplace as days passed. The sound of rain on the roof filled her head, and she could not tell waking from sleep. She saw her mother as though from a hawk's eyes far above, lying in her cot, a tiny dot in a sea of brittle yellow grass, praying. Teresa felt her own lips passing weakly over her mother's prayer, "with all its glories and sorrows, in reparation for all my sins..." She told Peanut, "Your grandmother had no gray hair when she died." Maybe Peanut was there to hear, and maybe not. Teresa saw the orphan girl, skinny arms wrapped around her distended belly. The girl watched her, saying nothing.

Hondo came one day. Teresa saw his beaten face gazing down at her, framed by dreads. He tried to smile, and when he could not quite manage it she knew he was really there.

"I need a favor," she told him. "A big favor." She smiled, thinking of the vegetables sealed in Mason jars, stacked nearly floor to ceiling in the basement. "*Pero puedo pagarle.*"

The rain stopped. The monsoons had broken, the air felt dry. Teresa sat up.

"Are you better now, Mama?" Peanut sat cross-legged on the floor beside her, surrounded by days' worth of squash and canta-loupe rinds.

Teresa did not answer. Instead she pulled herself from beneath sweat-soured blankets and stood on shaky legs. It was night, with a hint of autumn chill. "Let's clean up this garbage, Pea. Then it's time for bed." She lit the candle at the feet of the corncob Virgin Mother on the mantel and tucked Peanut in for the first time in days.

"Hondo's coming tomorrow," she said, touching Peanut's cheek. "Or maybe the day after. He's going to take you south on his wagon."

"Are you coming, too, Mama?" Peanut regarded Teresa with wide, serious eyes. Teresa stroked the girl's face.

"He's going to take the vegetables. But don't tell him about the seeds, baby. Those are yours. You leave them buried until you're old enough to come get them. Understand?"

"Okay, Mama."

"Promise?"

Peanut nodded. She shuddered with deep, quiet sobs. Teresa shushed her, stroked her hair, and softly began to sing. "*Una rata vieja que era planchadora...*" She sang until Peanut's sobs faded and the girl's chest rose and fell in the slow rhythm of sleep, and kept singing late into the night, pausing sometimes to cough and spit. She sang, rocking back and forth, until the lullaby's lyrics faded into her fevered exhaustion, and she had the strength left to sing only one word. Lupia. Lupia. Lupia.

About the Authors

MARGARET COEL is the author of thirteen novels in the Wind River mystery series and of five nonfiction books, including *Chief Left Hand*. Her latest novel is *Blood Memory*, set in Denver. She is a four-time winner of the Colorado Book Award, and recipient of the Women Writing the West Willa Award and the Left Coast Crime Conference's Rocky Award for Best Mystery Novel Set in the West. Her website is margaretcoel.com.

JOANNE GREENBERG is the author of thirteen novels, among them the best-selling *I Never Promised You a Rose Garden*, and four collections of short stories. She is the recipient of numerous awards, including the Frank Waters Award for Excellence in Writing and the Evil Companions Award. Greenberg has taught anthropology, ethics, and fiction writing at the Colorado School of Mines for twenty-five years.

PAM HOUSTON is the author of two linked short-story collections, *Cowboys Are My Weakness* and *Waltzing the Cat*; a novel, *Sight Hound*; and a collection of essays, *A Little More about Me.* She is director of creative writing at the University of California at Davis. Houston is the winner of the Western States Book Award, the Women Writing the West Willa Award, and the Evil Companions Literary Award.

NICK ARVIN is the author of *Articles of War*, the 2007 One Book, One Denver selection, and numerous short stories, including the collection *In the Electric Eden.* An engineer who works in power plant design, Arvin is the recipient of fellowships from the Michener-Copernicus Society, the Isherwood Foundation, and the National Endowment for the Arts. He is winner of the Colorado Book Award, the Rosenthal Foundation Award from the American Academy of Arts and Letters, and the Boyd Award from the American Library Association.

CONNIE WILLIS is the author of *Doomsday Book*, *To Say Nothing of the Dog*, *Passage*, *Bellwether*, and many other novels. Her most recent publication is *The Winds of Marble Arch*, a short story collection. She is the recipient of six Nebula Awards, presented by the Science Fiction Writers of America, and ten Hugo Awards, given by the World Science Fiction Convention, and is the only author to have won the awards in all four writing categories. She is also the winner of the American Library Association's Alex Award and the John W. Campbell Memorial Award and was named *Locus* magazine's science fiction writer of the decade.

SANDRA DALLAS, former bureau chief for *Business Week*, is the author of seven novels and ten nonfiction books. Her most recent novel, *Prayers for Sale*, was published in 2009. She is the recipient of the Cowboy Hall of Fame Wrangler Award and the Women Writing the West Willa Award and is a two-time winner of the Western Writers of America Spur Award.

MANUEL RAMOS is a lawyer and director of advocacy for Colorado Legal Services. A founder of *La Bloga*, an Internet magazine devoted to Latino literature, culture, news, and opinion, Ramos is the author of six crime novels, five featuring Denver lawyer Luis Móntez. He is the recipient of the Colorado Book Award and the Chicano/Latino Literary Award and was nominated for the Mystery Writers of America Edgar Award.

ARNOLD GROSSMAN, a former advertising creative director and political media consultant, coauthored two political novels with Colorado governor Richard D. Lamm. His latest book is *Going Together*, a quirky novel set in Los Angeles. A cofounder of SAFE Colorado, which sponsored a successful Colorado initiative to close the gun-show loophole, he also wrote *One Nation Under Guns: An Essay on an American Epidemic.*

ROBERT GREER is the author of seven books in the CJ Floyd mystery series, two medical thrillers, a short story collection, and his latest novel, *Spoon*. He is a practicing surgical pathologist, research scientist, and professor of medicine and pathology at the University of Colorado Denver Anschutz Medical Campus.

DIANE MOTT DAVIDSON is a *New York Times* best-selling author of fourteen culinary mysteries, all featuring her amateur sleuth, caterer Goldy Schulz. Her latest novel is *Sweet Revenge*. She is the recipient of Bouchercon's Anthony Award and was named Writer of the Year by Rocky Mountain Fiction Writers.

LAURA PRITCHETT is the author of a novel, *Sky Bridge*, and a collection of short stories, *Hell's Bottom, Colorado*. She is coeditor of three nonfiction books, including her most recent, *The Gleaners: Eco Essays on Recycling, Re-Use, and Living Lightly on the Land*. She is the winner of the Colorado Book Award, the Women Writing the West Willa Award, the PEN USA Award, and the Milkweed National Fiction Prize.

ROBERT POGUE ZIEGLER is a freelance journalist and copy editor who has previously published short stories in small magazines and is at work on a science fiction novel. Ziegler lives in Paonia with his wife and son. He often writes under the pen name Robert Pogue.

About the Artwork

After traveling along Larimer Street from the Tivoli to Downing Street, I had three thoughts that I felt should be the parameters in creating the illustrations for this series:

First was to convey the spirit of the story. There are visual elements from each story, in some form, in its illustration. Some are quite literal, others more metaphorical.

Second was to use images solely from Larimer Street—good and bad. Over a period of a couple of weeks I was able to take more than five hundred photographs to choose from to create the illustrations.

Third was to attempt to portray the period of time from my personal, albeit fluid, interpretation of art history.

Each illustration is essentially a kind of multiple exposure. Each was made from at least three photographs taken along Larimer Street that were assembled in PhotoShop on individual layers. Each layer was then manipulated in a variety of ways—color, saturation, and its interaction with the other layers above and below.

—Charles Chamberlin